MY TUTOR, MY STALKER

JADE SWALLOW

Copyright © 2024 by Jade Swallow

All rights reserved.

No part of this book may be reproduced in any form or by any electronic or mechanical means, including information storage and retrieval systems, without written permission from the author, except for the use of brief quotations in a book review.

CONTENTS

Content Warnings	v
1. Ronan	1
2. Elsie	10
3. Ronan	30
4. Elsie	44
5. Ronan	51
6. Elsie	59
7. Ronan	68
8. Elsie	77
9. Ronan	87
About the Author	97
Also by Jade Swallow	99

CONTENT WARNINGS

This book contains a forbidden erotic relationship between two consenting adults and is intended for readers over 18.

A non-exhaustive list of content includes: Stalking, relationship with a stalker, breeding kink with lots of unprotected sex, tutor stalker romance, morally gray hero, FMC in high school, mentions of physical abuse, death of a loved one (off-page), degradation and praise, dirty talking, pregnancy, pregnant sex (with a baby bump), lactation kink (adult milking), mild Daddy kink with the use of words 'Daddy' and 'Babygirl', dubcon, and typos and grammatical errors.

Please note this is a work of fiction featuring imaginary scenarios. Only read if you are comfortable with the above themes. The author does not endorse the beliefs or actions of the characters.

If you read this book anywhere other than Amazon, you have an illegal pirated copy. I encourage you to research the harmful effects of piracy on authors and obtain a legal copy instead. Thanks.

CHAPTER 1
RONAN

She's so beautiful.

With blonde hair framing her smiling oval face, Elsie Mulligan is an angel who's caught the attention of the devil. Her clear blue eyes twinkle as she gazes at the camera I've planted in her bookcase, oblivious that I'm watching her. Orange light falls on her face, framing her lush lips, and small nose, and sliding down those beautiful tits that are half-exposed in her black tank top. With her phone in hand, she raises the camera to frame her face and make her perky tits appear deeper. Then, she pulls down the neck of her top and pouts at the camera.

Click.

She's taking pictures of herself.

I inhale a heavy breath, struggling not to recall her vanilla and caramel scent as I watch her pull down her tank another notch. This time, a pink nipple almost pops out of it, making my cock twitch in response. With a wicked smile, Elsie clicks another picture of her half-naked, her thighs pressing together in her teeny-tiny pajama shorts. They barely cover her ass, cupping her mound so tight that I can see the outline of her delicate pussy lips.

"Mmmm…" Slowly, I bring my hand to my cock and start stroking.

I'm sitting in my dorm room, music blasting outside the window. Some students are screaming and dancing, drunk from the frat party going on downstairs. My room is dark, my screen flashing bright with an image of the woman who takes my breath away—Elsie Mulligan. She's my student, my secret fantasy, and my ultimate revenge.

Ping.

My phone lights up with a text.

My hand immediately reaches for it, and when I flip my phone, the image of Elsie in her tank with her nipple out greets me. My eyes almost pop at the sight, wondering what's suddenly made her lose control.

Elsie: Good evening, Mr. Jackson. I hope you're having a good night. Here's a little something to make you feel better.

My stomach clenches, my eyes boring into the image of Elsie's exposed tits. I've never seen her nipples before, but damn, they're all perky and pink and hard, making me want to rip off her clothes and suckle on them.

I've been tutoring her for two years and though her grades have gone up in that time, so has her boldness. She's always been the cheerful one of us both. When she confessed that she liked me at sixteen, I brushed her off as a teenager with a crush on her tutor. But we both know my feelings for her run a lot deeper than that.

My eyes flicker to the image of a teenage boy on my desk, the video of Elsie still playing on my laptop. My big brother. I inhale a deep breath, realizing why I'm doing this.

"Levi." I close my eyes, trying to remind myself of the horrible night my brother died. Memories of his painful suicide linger in my heart five years after it happened. I was sixteen back then and I knew something was wrong with my older brother. We were only a year apart and that made us close. Well, as close as brothers can be. So, when he came home from school one day with a cut on his wrist, I knew something was wrong.

I watch the image of my late brother, his silver eyes that are identical to mine squinting behind his glasses as he smiles. He got into Harvard, but he never got to go. I wonder what things would be like if it had been him instead of me sitting in this dorm room. Would he have had his first experience with a girl? Would he be terrorizing other smart kids with his math skills? We'll never know because it's me sitting in his place, getting a degree in math I'm not even passionate about. And it's all thanks to George Mulligan. Elsie's brother.

My fist grips the edge of my desk hard as another message lights up my screen.

Elsie: Do you think this one's nicer? I think this angle shows off my assets better.

Elsie's tank top hangs under her breasts, both her nipples on full display. I suck in a ragged breath, unable to stop my body from responding to her. I wish we weren't tangled up in this twisted revenge, because she's not just someone I tutor, she's my obsession.

Stroking my cock with one hand, I type out a reply with another.

Ronan: You're a spoiled little brat. Just go to sleep and stop sending strange men pics of your bosom.

It's a regular reply, one I'm conditioned to give as her tutor. I don't glance back at my brother's image, feeling a trickle of guilt for getting hard for his bully's sister.

Closing my eyes, I recall the day I came back home to find my brother dead in his bedroom. He'd taken an entire bottle of pills. Next to him was a handwritten note that said, 'I can't take it anymore.'. My whole world went blank as I realized what had happened. I called 911 and Mom rushed back from work, but we were both too late. Levi was gone by the time he arrived at the hospital.

Mom cried, but I just felt so lost. I'd noticed the signs,

noticed that something was off with Levi. Ever since he'd started his sophomore year, he'd become paranoid and jittery. When I asked him, he said it was just the stress from all the studying. He was taking extra credits and working hard to get into Harvard. He was elated when he got the admission letter, but soon, I began noticing signs of stress. I didn't know why he was so depressed, but when I told Mom about it, she tried taking him to a therapist. However, Levi refused to go after the first time, saying he was fine.

It was only after he died that I discovered why he'd taken his life.

Elsie: OMG, you didn't really say 'bosom'. What is this, Victorian England?

I breathe out, trying to distract myself with Elsie's body when the pain hit. After Levi's death, I'd felt powerless, lost even. I studied harder, knowing he wanted us to go to Harvard together. However, when I realized why my brother had taken his life, everything changed.

Ronan: It's midnight. Go to bed.

Elsie: Why? Do you wanna join me there?

When I don't reply, she sends another message.

Elsie: And you're not a strange man. You're my tutor. We meet every weekend, remember?

Yes, the tutoring. I gaze at the calendar on my wall, counting the days I've tutored Elsie. It started as a plan for revenge. I wanted to get closer to George, her brother.

One of Levi's classmates told me that George was bullying him. He wanted to get into Harvard too, but when he didn't make it, he took his anger out on Levi. It'd been that way since he transferred to our school. Everyone knew George was a rich, spoiled brat, one who'd daddy spent a lot of money covering up his vices. What I didn't know was that he'd been bullying my brother for being a nerd, for getting something he could never have. He hurt him, and ruthlessly bullied him until he was alone. My brother was targeted and hurt, and he had to go through all of that alone. The unfairness of it makes my blood heat every time I think about it. Being a rich kid, George got away with it. Nobody could stop him, and Levi had to pay the price.

Ronan: That's the only reason I'm not spanking your naughty ass until it welts. Do you know photos like this can come back to haunt you when you're older?

Elsie: Oh, I didn't know you're into BDSM. Maybe we can try it sometime. I'm eighteen now;)

I shut my eyes, trying to block out the temptation of her, but I'm too weak. My eyes are riveted to her beautiful body, studying every inch of her soft, smooth skin. Her movements are hypnotic, making me forget my sole purpose in life—revenge.

After I realized what George had done to my brother, I wanted to get back at him. His father had known that he was responsible, yet, he hushed it up. Only Mom and I were the victims of his cruelty. I wanted to hurt him, to make him feel what it felt like when someone you loved was hurt. And that someone had to be Elsie.

I made meticulous plans to get close to her, signing up to be her tutor when I realized her parents were looking for someone to help her with math. My experience getting into a top college impressed them and they decided I was the best option for the job. And just like that, I was in the Mulligans' circle. I kept an eye on George and Elsie's dad, picturing their faces when I destroyed their precious little princess. Her dad was just as responsible as George for hushing things up, and he was going to pay with his daughter's future. At first, I wanted to kill George for what he'd done, but this was much better, much sweeter. I wasn't just going to fuck up her chances of going to college, I was going to fuck up her life and bring shame to the Mulligan family. And then, I was going to leave her.

However, the one thing I hadn't planned on was my

attraction to Elsie.

Elsie: And I don't really care. I know you're too uptight to ever share photos of me.

Uptight? She has no idea that I'm watching her right now, stroking my cock as she rolls the hem of her tank top up. My little dove doesn't know that even now, I'm picturing what it'd feel like to sink my thick cock into her virgin pussy and feel it stretch for me. Would she scream when I pop her cherry and make her come? Would she moan my name when I fill her with my cum and breed her? Or would she take it all like a good girl and grow my baby in her stomach? The visual of that flat stomach growing round with my seed sends a flash of heat through my core.

My fist tightens on my bulge when her top disappears, leaving her naked from the waist up. Her tits are high and firm, topped with two hard little pink tips. Elsie circles one aroused nipple with her thumb, moaning when she feels a spark of pleasure.

I grunt in my room, pulling down the waistband of my sweatpants and finding my swelling cock inside. My balls feel tight as I watch my little bratty student put on a show, thumbing and stroking her breasts as I pump my cock in rhythm to the movement of those delicate fingers. I don't have to see them to know she hasn't worked a day in her life. Being the daughter of Robert Mulligan, one of the richest investment bankers in town, her life is one of financial ease.

Elsie: P.S. Maybe we should make a sex tape so that it gets shared online. Maybe then you'd stop being so serious.

I let out an exasperated sigh. She has no idea about all the things I plan to do with that nubile body of hers. I've been holding onto my self-control for years, making her long for me to the point she'd do anything to be mine.

However, the stalking wasn't part of my plan. It's simply

for my pleasure. I want to make sure Elsie is safe until I come for her. That's what I told myself when I planted those cameras, but months later, it's clear that my feelings for her are way deeper than a passing fancy.

Ronan: Good night.

Elsie leans over the phone, reading my message with pensive brows. But as she does, I notice the familiar lines on her back. Red and brown that have welted to purple. My fist tightens and I move it over my cock, feeling her pain wash through me. Elsie might be a spoiled rich princess, but the reason I haven't destroyed her yet is because I know that she's just a prisoner in a golden cage. When I planned out my revenge, I hadn't planned on being faced with a dilemma like this. Instead of ruining her, I want to ruin her family for hurting her.

Her mom has a drinking problem and sometimes, she gets violent. Her dad also has expectations from her and when she failed to get into Harvard last year, I know her hit her. My throat retches violently at the thought of another man putting his hands on my little dove with the intent to hurt. She might be flirty and bratty, but I know she only does it because she can't breathe in that house. She wants freedom, attention, and the love her parents have never given her. It's the reason she keeps her back hidden during class. They are scars she hides from me.

Elsie leans over her camera, exposing more of those healing scars to me. I want to kiss them, to make her feel better.

My phone flashes bright again and my eyes burn with the image of her bare tits hanging loose over the phone screen. I want to nip and suck on them while she leans over me, making her ride my big cock as I taste those pretty tits. Pre-cum leaks from my cock, making my stroke harder. I feel tension rise in the base of my spine, aching for release.

Elsie: Do you like this one better? I feel responsible for filling up your spank bank. Life must be so dull just studying math all day.

I can't spare any hands to write a reply so I just watch her jiggle her tits on camera and move her ass while she frowns at the phone. Just watching her like that is enough to make my body surrender. With a final hard stroke, I climax in my pants, drenching them in cum. All the passion I keep hidden explodes out of me, taking me high to a place that only she can. I close my eyes and feel my release fill up my body. The pleasure is painful, a reminder of the forbidden attraction I share with the girl I'm stalking. I let the sensation consume my body until I'm too tired to think of all the reasons we're wrong together, of all the pain that separates us. When I finish climaxing, she's sent me three more messages. More pictures of those tempting titties that are all hard and eager for me.

Elsie: Do you like sucking, Mr. Jackson? Because I know I do.

I don't even count how many ways that sentence can be interpreted before I fire off the first thought that comes to my mind.

Ronan: Do your parents know you flash your tits like a slut for your tutor?

I press 'send' before I can delete those words. I know I'm crossing the line with this one, but it's gone before I can think. No reply comes immediately, but when I look at the screen, I see Elsie moaning and biting her lower lip.

Elsie: Do you talk dirty like that to all your students?

No, only you.

Ronan: Only ones that send me nude pics at midnight.

Elsie: It's called sexting. I'm sure people of your generation do it too.

I scoff. We're only three years apart but she treats me like I'm forty because I don't give in to her advances. It's kinda cute.

Ronan: I'll see you tomorrow. With all your clothes on. I hope you've done your homework.

Elsie: Did you have to ruin it with the mention of homework?
Ronan: Good night, Elsie.

And then, I turn over the phone and slump over my chair. It looks like it might be time to proceed to the next phase of my plan—Breeding Elsie.

CHAPTER 2
ELSIE

I'm tapping my pen on my deck when I hear the doorbell ring. Instantly, I'm on my feet, knowing that he is here. My body instantly lights up, the thought of my tempting, older private math tutor sending flutters down my core. I glance out of the window, spying his mop of dark brown hair as it disappears inside the door.

Last night, I pushed the boundaries by sending him pictures of my tits. I know it is bad and naughty, and I know he's never obviously expressed any interest in me, but he's the only silver lining in my life. Mom got drunk last night and she loves using her leash on me when she's violent, recounting how I ruined her figure and my parents' marriage. It's not my fault that Dad cheated on her because she gained weight, but it's what we believe in this family. I know my parents care for me and Dad spoils me with so many luxurious things. Still, I wish they loved me too, loved me enough to get through their issues.

With George away at college, I am in a precarious position. After my brother failed to get into any prestigious institutions despite Dad giving them big donations, the expectations shifted to me. After I failed to get in despite my improved SAT score, Dad got serious. Last night, things got really awkward when my parents announced their plans for my future.

"You're getting married as soon as you graduate school," Mom said, half-drunk. I thought she was kidding, but then, I turned to Dad who looked utterly serious.

"Your brother has already disappointed us by not getting into an Ivy League school. I hope you're not planning to follow in his footsteps." I got admission letters from a bunch of universities last year and none of them were the ones my Dad wanted. Despite hiring a tutor for me, I'd failed to meet his expectations.

"But Dad, you said you wanted me to go to college."

"Not anymore. The Kingstons, you know the family, Bill and you are classmates." My heart stopped beating when he mentioned Bill because he was the most boring person I knew. Bill was a spoiled, rich kid just like my brother, and he only knew how to waste his life until his parents handed him the reins of their banking empire. I had no doubt he'd cheat on me as soon as he went to college and treat me like an accessory as soon as I delivered the prescribed 2.5 kids. I didn't want that kind of life for myself, not after I'd grown up in a household where my parents barely tolerated each other and stuck together only for appearances. "Well, Bill is going to Yale next Fall and he wants to marry you."

"What!? Dad, I'm only eighteen. I'm too young to get married." I had planned on going to college and falling in love after I graduated high school. I wanted to find someone who loved me for who I was and not for my family connections.

"Your mother was nineteen when we got married. You're not that young anymore. Bill wants to meet you next week so that his parents and I can come to an agreement. I hope you'll show up in your best clothes." Dad's voice was harsh and I knew he'd hit me if I didn't listen. Dad didn't usually hit me, but it happened every once in a while when I failed to meet his expectations. After my disappointing admission letters, I stopped arguing with him. "And while we're at it, I think it's time you stopped getting private tuitions. Your math grades are up and you don't need to study so hard anymore."

My heart dropped like a stone. The thought of being stuck with my parents and never seeing Ronan again was the worst kind of punishment.

"No! Please. I promise I'll behave but let me get private tuition until I graduate." I never thought I'd be begging my parents to let me study. My hot tutor was the only ray of hope in my life. "You said that studying Ronan was having a positive effect on my grades."

"I can't believe vermin like him gets to study at a prestigious institution while my children bring nothing but disappointment to the Mulligan name." Dad stands up. "Fine, you can have your math classes but don't think that's going to get you out of a marriage with Bill."

With that, he left.

That's why I sent Ronan those tit pics. I wanted to do something bad and naughty before I signed my life away to a lifetime of maintaining appearances. I want to be loved and desired by a hard-working, capable man like Ronan. I've been in love with him since the day he walked in through the door and said he'd be teaching me math. He was so serious, but he was stable and caring, something my parents had never been. With him, I felt like I wasn't drowning. I could be myself, tease him, play with him, and he'd let me. But there is one line he never crosses.

There's a knock on the door.

"Come in." My eyes are glued to the door that opens, revealing the tall, dark, and handsome form of my private tutor. He steps in, taking up space in the room, and making my heart speed up. Ronan has been my tutor for two years, but I feel like this every time I see him.

"Good evening," his voice is deep and sexy, seeping into my heart like medicine. The invisible pressure I've been feeling all day dissolves and my heart feels a little lighter.

Ronan Jackson is sexy AF. With those stormy, broody silver eyes, thick brown hair, a sharp jaw lined with stubble, and the hardest body I've seen, he's my version of a porn video. At over six feet, he's tall and athletic, his figure a mismatch to his intellectual personality. I still can't believe he's studying Math with a body like that when he could be using it to make women come instead. He should be a model or a football player.

"Good evening, Elsie." He's all formal in that crisp white shirt he insists on wearing to our tutoring sessions. I know he wears a t-shirt and hoodies like normal guys at college, but he acts like I'm a job when he's here. I know Dad pays him to make sure I pass all my classes, but my feelings for my tutor are nowhere near professional. His gaze flickers over the books on the table, my bookshelf, and my bed with a crumpled pink bedsheet that was part of the pics I sent him last night. I'm wearing a half-sleeve V-neck t-shirt and a push-up bra that tries too hard to show off my assets. I know men like girls with big boobs, but no matter how many YouTube breast-enhancing massages I try, my tits won't grow. Ronan's gaze slides down my chest, taking in my miniskirt that barely covers my ass. I wear clothes like that to tempt him, but deep down, I just want him to love me. Ronan is the only person who listens to me, the only one who replies to my messages and gives me attention. I notice the slight difference in his breathing, feeling a sense of accomplishment when he turns his gaze away. "Shall we start today's lesson?"

"I know you don't speak like that to your friends." I went

to view Ronan's college because Dad wanted me to go there but instead of seeing the buildings, my eyes were fixed on my hot, older tutor.

"How do you know that?" His silver eyes narrow. "Have you been stalking me?"

The mention of that word makes my pussy quiver. Ronan's narrowed eyes make me feel like I'm the only woman in the world. I wish he'd stalk me, see me every time I slipped my fingers between my legs in the sanctuary of my bedroom and came calling out his name. My cheeks heat, realizing how disturbing my fantasies are.

I shrug. "I bet there isn't much to you except Math and studying." I want to appear nonchalant, to label him as a boring person so that I can get on with my life. But no matter how hard I try to convince myself, my body won't stop wanting him. I feel there's a hidden depth to him, a shadowy beast he keeps under lock and key. How else could someone who looks that hot not be interested in girls?

There's a flash of something in Ronan's eyes but then, he turns away and begins pulling out his books. He sits down on the chair next to me, placing them on the table as I take my seat. Just sitting next to him and talking about math feels intimate. "Did you do your homework?"

"Not all of it. I was busy sexting last night." His fingers pause when I mention that word. I pull my chair closer to my tutor. "Did you like the pics I sent?"

"I deleted them."

"Awww, that's so tragic. How are you going to get through college sex? Surely, even you need relief sometimes. My brother says men that age need release. They can't stay with the same woman for too long."

Ronan grips the book a little too tight, making me wonder if he hates men who cheat. I bet he'd never cheat if he had a girlfriend. I've asked him about it, but he says he's too busy to date. I know Ronan works several part-time jobs including this one to make ends meet. He doesn't come from one and though he has a scholarship and his mom helps him out, he still needs to make money. I might've been a sheltered princess all my life but there's something about a hardworking man like Ronan that turns me on. He isn't like my brother or Bill. He worked for everything he'd got and that makes him so much sexier.

"When I go to college, I plan to sleep with a new guy every week. Just to keep things interesting."

Ronan's chest rises and falls unevenly, making me wonder if I finally got to him. He doesn't seem like the jealous type, but maybe I'm wrong. "College is for studying, not sleeping with boys."

I sense it every time he holds himself back. It's like he adorns the mask of a stern tutor when he could be so much more. There's a simmering passion beneath his surface,

"Where's the fun in all work and no play?" I slide my palm over Ronan's thigh and feel a muscle jump underneath. "Don't you ever want to play?" I turn my voice into a seductive purr. We've been playing this game for years, and he never melts. Still, I won't stop trying. "You know, kiss a girl or make out? Go to parties, get drunk, wake up naked in bed with someone you don't even know."

"No." There's a burning intensity in his gaze as he says it. How can a man like this be single? It's not even logical. I know girls at his college are all over him.

I snuggle closer, my breasts brushing against his side as I whisper in his ear, "What about someone you know?"

His hand moves, grabbing my back in an attempt to pull me away, but as he does, I flinch.

"Ouch." I try to pull away, but Ronan stops me by grabbing my wrist. His eyes meet mine and I look down, trying to avoid my weakness.

"Are you hurt somewhere?" his voice is steady, making my nerves buzz.

"No. It was just—" He pulls me closer, fisting the hem of my top and yanking it up to reveal the scars on my back. He pushes the fabric up my spine, revealing inches of scarred skin. I close my eyes, feeling the air cool the marks on my back. Mom makes me submit to her wishes when she's really angry, and that's usually every time she gets a picture of Dad and his secretary from her private investigator. I don't even know why she has one, but she spends all day crying over it, drinking herself to death. When I try to interfere, she blames me and hits me.

"Are those..." His eyes go wide with fury as he takes in my scars. I feel exposed and ashamed. I didn't ever want him to see me like this. It doesn't take a genius to figure out where they came from. Ronan has seen my mother drink. She even came onto him once but he refused her. Then, she threw glasses around and created a mess until the maids made her stop. Ronan runs his thumb over the new scar and I moan. "Is this the one that I touched?"

He's so cool, so calm and collected despite the rage I know he feels.

"Yes." He's holding me too close. I'm half in love with my tutor though he's never shown any interest in me before. But Ronan is the only one who ever listens to me. With him by my side, I feel a little less lonely.

Time stands still as he drags his finger over the healing mark, making me breathe heavier with each stroke. His fingers tighten on my wrist, digging into my flesh so hard that I think it'll break. He's never been so forceful with me before, never tried to do anything like this, and I kinda like it.

"You're...hurting me."

His head snaps up and Ronan immediately loosens his grip. "I'm sorry."

"You should let me go before someone walks in. The door

isn't locked, remember?" My voice is breathy, his touches making my pussy moist and ready.

"Do you have scars anywhere else?" I can't stop my body from reacting to his touches, can't stop the anticipation in my heart when he treats me with kindness.

"A few in my thigh, stomach, and neck, though they've faded." Mom tried to strangle me once when she was really angry but Dad came and broke us up. She went to rehab for a bit after that, but she still has an alcohol addiction. I know she only does it because she's sad, but I want her to stop.

"Turn around." I obey him, turning my body so that he can get a clearer view of my back. Ronan pulls my shirt up, tugging on my hands. I raise them, allowing him to take them off my body, leaving me in only my white t-shirt bra, and miniskirt. I feel so exposed, though he's seen me in far less than this. Coiling a hand around my stomach, he pulls me toward him. His lips ghost my ear, his fingers touching the marks on my back, opening me up in a way nobody else ever has. "Who hurt you, little dove?"

Little dove.

He calls me that sometimes. And I love it. It makes me feel special.

I moan when Ronan runs his calloused thumb over one welt, gently touching it. My entire body turns into a puddle, leaning into his touch.

"Who did this to your beautiful body?" There's no mistaking the raw possessiveness, the undisguised anger in his voice.

"You think I'm beautiful?" My flirtation is my defense mechanism. I don't want him to dig too deep, to know how imperfect I am on the inside.

"Answer me. Was it your mom?" I sense him shift, his knuckle stroking my spine all the way to where the waistband of my skirt is. My nipples tighten under my bra, aching to be touched by those big, rough hands.

"Yes...It's nothing out of the ordinary." I sense him shifting, just stifling a yelp when he picks me up like a doll and slides me over his muscular thigh. I'm about to say something when I feel his thick, massive erection under my ass, poking through my skirt. I forget to breathe, closing my eyes and reveling in the sensation of sitting on my hot tutor's lap and being touched by him.

Lowering his head, he whispers against my skin, "I want to kill your parents for hurting you. You're not even safe in your own home." I've never seen such a display of emotion from him before. Has Ronan been hurt too? Is that why he's so concerned about me.

When I feel him move, I ask, "What are you doing?"

"Making you feel better."

Ronan's lips brush against my broken skin, cutting off all my thoughts. He moves his lips over my wound, kissing it lovingly. My mind melts because no one has done anything like that before, and my body loves it. I love how careful he is, giving me scars attention as he kisses them one by one. The feelings I've buried in my heart explode. I grab his arm where it flexes around my waist, needing this so much. When I sent him those pics last night, I wanted him to touch me, to suckle on my tits like I was more than a student to him. I want him to be the first man who touches me, the one who takes my virginity and makes me his. But this is so much better. It's like he knows exactly what I need.

"Ronan..." My pussy clenches around the air. His hot breath mists against my skin, my nipples tingling for my hot tutor. I let him touch my healed marks, kissing each and every one until my pussy is hot and hungry for more. My ass slides against his bulge, my whole body aching for my tutor. I know this is so wrong. He could get into trouble if Dad ever found out what we did, but I still want him.

He finishes kissing my scars one by one, keeping me securely in his lap. I lose myself in his kisses, needing him so bad. I want his cock inside me, his mouth on my tits making me forget the pain.

A loud crash outside the door makes us both sit up. I hear my mom screaming downstairs and roll off Ronan's lap in a second. She's been drinking again and she's getting violent. I reach for the door handle but Ronan gets there first, placing his hand over mine.

"Don't go." His voice is firm. Ronan pushes me against the door, caging me with his tall, big body. His hands reach over my head and he bolts the door. "She'll only hurt you more."

"But…she…"

"Let the servants deal with it. They've been through it before." I don't know how he knows that. Probably from the last time she lost her temper. "It's not your responsibility, Elsie." His hand slides down my shoulder, touching the soft skin of my arm. His eyes are two molten pools of silver, blazing fiercely as I swallow. I want him so bad. Ronan leans forward, kissing my shoulder. "Tell me what happened yesterday." His thumb strokes my clavicle as he kisses my neck, and my jaw, trailing his hot lips over my cheek. My pussy leaks moisture, coating my seam. I don't have to touch my panties to know that they're soaked. "Why did you send me those pics? You've never done anything like that before."

"I…" I want to lie to him, say something a sophisticated woman would. However, the truth bursts out of my lips. "My parents want me to get married as soon as I graduate."

"What?" The surprise in Ronan's voice is unmistakable. He pulls back, gazing into my eyes and there's no hiding the worry in my eyes. "You don't want to get married."

"No, I'm only eighteen." I close my eyes. "But that isn't the only reason. Bill…he's George's friend and he…let's just say I can't see myself falling in love with him."

"You're a major. They can't force you into it."

"I'm also financially dependent on my parents and

without a college degree, I'll continue to be. It was going to happen sooner or later."

"But it's not what you want." His words are firm, and relentless, forcing me to face my desires. I inhale and exhale roughly as the sounds downstairs fade. My breasts rise and fall before my tutor's eyes. He brings his face close to me, his lips hovering just an inch from mine. My eyes drop to his mouth, wanting so bad to close the distance and kiss him.

"What do you want, Elsie?"

"I...I...." I gaze into his stormy eyes, knowing that if I don't do this now, I never will. "I want you, Ronan. I want you to take my virginity."

Ronan growls. "You don't know what you're asking for, Elsie."

I shake my head. "I know you're older than me and I'm just a kid to you, but I've...I've been into you for a while. I want my first time to be with you. Please, I want to know what it feels like to be desired. The way you look at your books when you're focused....I want you to look at me like that."

My words are the immature desires of a teenage girl who's in too deep, but Ronan doesn't belittle me or brush me away like he usually does. Instead, he places his hands on my hips and gazes deep into my eyes, making me go all hot. Yeah, that's exactly how I want my future husband to look at me like I'm the only woman in the world.

"I don't share, baby girl." My heart skips a beat. He's never called me 'baby girl' before but I love it. "If I take your virginity, I will come inside you and make you mine. You'll be bred before you can blink."

Bred.

The word coils around my head like a poisonous vine.

I've never thought about getting pregnant. Though I knew I'd eventually have kids, I never believed it would be a pleasurable process. But doing it with Ronan...I lick my

MY TUTOR, MY STALKER 21

lips. The thought of being knocked up by my tutor, of carrying his baby and caressing my stomach when it's round and full, is a wet dream. He must've seen the expression on my face for he adds, "Damn it, you like that idea, don't you?"

The cat got my tongue because I can't admit to it. "I don't care if I get pregnant. Please, just make me feel better."

He hears my desperate plea for one moment I'm standing against the door and the next, I'm being thrown on my bed. My back hits the soft, pink mattress, my tits bouncing.

Ronan climbs over me, caging my hips with his thighs and gazing down at me. "Are you sure you won't regret this?" His hands reach forward and cup my breasts, gently kneading them through my bra. He slips his thumb under the cup, stroking my hard nipple, and I moan in response.

"Never. I want you to be my first, Ronan." Our eyes lock for a second and I know he's considering my request.

I'm almost convinced he's going to reject me when he says, "I'll do it, but not tonight. You're not ready for it yet." My heart deflates with disappointment but his hands slide out, reaching for the back of my bra. "But I am going to make you come tonight. I'll give you an orgasm to remember." I arch my back, presenting my breasts to him as he finds the buckle and snaps it open. My breasts sag when the bra loosens. Using his big hands, Ronan pulls it off. And then, I'm naked from the waist up, just like last night.

Ronan stares at my bared breasts for a whole minute, making me feel self-conscious. Are they too small for him? Does he like them bigger? Did they look better in the photos?"

My crush hisses. "Fuck, you're going to kill me. I've been dreaming of sucking on those pink nipples since you sent me those photos last night." His finger brushes over one beaded peak. "They're even better in real life." His eyes are revering, making me feel so desired. Ronan drops his head, bringing his mouth to one hard peak. Then, he closes his lips around my tips and suckles.

"Aaahhh..." My toes curl as a flash of heat fills my body, spiraling down my breasts to my core. Ronan's lips are sexy and perfect, suckling on my little bud ardently. He rolls his tongue over my nipple, making my pussy flood with moisture. His other hand squeezes my bare breast, plumping it before taking my little nipple in his fingers and rolling it around. "Ronan..." My body surrenders to him, my arms going around him to hold him close to my heart. He's unraveling me with every suck and lick. When his teeth rub against my sensitive areola, I cry out.

Instantly, Ronan stops suckling on my breast and looks up. "You've gotta keep your voice down if you don't want us to be discovered." He rolls his tongue over my other nipple that's a little red from his playing. "I don't want this to end before I've had the chance to taste your pussy."

I swallow my aching body struggling to maintain control. He makes me feel so much at once. I can't believe Ronan is fully clothed when I'm mostly naked. He suckles my other peak and this time, I stuff a pillow over my face when he lightly bites on my nipple flooding my body with white-hot heat. I've never felt like this before. The air is saturated with Ronan's masculine scent, the feel of this mouth over my tits making the ache between my legs intensify. When he sucks hard on my nipple, I scream into my pillow.

"Good girl." He squeezes my other breast as he kisses the one he's been pleasuring. He pulls his head back and takes the pillow off my face. "You look so pretty when you're blushing for me. I want to kiss you so bad right now."

"Do it," I say, raising my hands. "I've wanted you for so long."

With a grunt, Ronan covers my mouth with his. My heart explodes into fireworks when our lips meet, the bliss spreading all over my aroused body. Ronan's hands reach for my skirt zipper and pull it down, leaving me in just my panties. His hands slide over my bare thighs, making my pussy drip for him. I moan into his mouth and loop my arms around his neck, feeling him close to me as he deepens the kiss. His mouth consumes me, igniting a deep need in my core. His hands move up my belly, caressing my hips before my cups one breast and gently kneads it.

Ronan thrusts his tongue into my mouth, one hand slipping between my thighs. His fingers brush the wet spot in my panties, teasing my puffy folds. He moans into my mouth, his tongue intertwining with mine as he pushes the fabric at my crotch aside and presses a textured digit over my bare, dripping folds. I cry into his mouth, the sensation of my hot tutor touching my cunt making me go crazy. He uses his other finger to pluck one nipple and roll it between two fingers as his mouth devours me. Feeling him touching those forbidden places is pure fantasy. I can't believe we're making out in my parents' house, while my mother is screaming downstairs. His burning kiss is the escape I need, the only thing that can make me forget reality.

I close my eyes, surrendering to his passionate mouth as it explores and arouses me. His fingers slide up and down my slit, pausing at my clit and gently rubbing it. A shockwave passes through my core. A climax begins to build inside me.

"Ronan…" I break the kiss, gasping for air.

"I want to see you naked, Elsie. I wanna touch you where nobody else has ever touched you." He tears my panties away with a feral growl, our bodies aching to be joined. I feel his bulge brush against my thigh when he sits back down. Pushing my thighs open, he gazes mesmerized at my bare pussy. My mound is clean-shaven. I shave it every week hoping Ronan will see it. He runs his knuckles over my moist folds, making butterflies flutter in my belly.

"Such a pretty little pussy. Are you this wet every time we have a lesson?"

"Yes…I'm always hot for you." His fingers travel up and down, making me needier. I arch my back up, pushing my tits in the air.

"I want to fill this blushing little cunt with my cock until you're bleeding all over me." His voice is rough as he uses his fingers to circle my cunt that's steadily leaking. "Just the thought of coming inside you and filling you up with my cum makes me hard."

"Mmmm…" I can't hold back how hot my body gets when he says dirty things about breeding me. Maybe I should let him knock me up so that I can get out of this engagement with Bill.

"When I pop your cherry, it'll be in my bed. An unhurried, slow, lovemaking that'll last all night. I'll make you come so many times you'll be too sore to walk the next day. I'll keep you in my bed the next day and lick that sore pussy until it's feeling better."

Oh my god. He's making dirty promises to me, reassuring me that he wants me, even though he isn't taking my virginity right now. There's a loud scream downstairs and I'm worried my mom will walk in, but Ronan just squeezes my thigh and slips lower. He's reading my mind and he knows I'm anxious. The way he responds to my tiniest emotion is amazing. When his face slips between my legs, his hot breaths falling on my bare sex, I swallow.

"Mmm…it's time to eat this pussy." He sticks his thick, wet tongue out, licking my slit in a slow, long stroke. My cunt pulses in response, pleasure unfurling in my core.

"Ronan…." My legs shake as my fingers reach for his hair, gripping his dark brown mane desperately.

"You smell so sweet when you're all aroused and ready to come." His vocal vibrations echo in my pussy. He flicks his tongue against my seam, stimulating me. When he flicks his tip on my clit, the pulses inside my belly turn more violent.

"Your clit is so hard and needy for my mouth, little dove. Do you want me to make it feel better?"

"Yes, please." I am begging him.

Ronan captures my little button between his lips and lightly pulls. My bad arches, another scream exploding from my mouth as he sucks on my fleshy little clit. My mind melts as rapture shoots up my sex, a buzz beginning to build inside me.

"Hold those tits up for me, little dove. I want you to play with the nipples that I just sucked on while I make you come."

His dirty commands are impossible to refute so I grab my tits in my little hands and begin rolling my nipples around between french manicured fingers. Ronan sucks my clit again, but this time, he lightly teases it with the edge of his teeth. His torturous sucking coupled with my fingers takes my pleasure to the next level.

"I am going to come…" I cry out, every tug and pull on my clit making me lose control.

"Not so fast, baby. I still haven't tasted that sweet cunt." Ronan opens his mouth and releases my swollen clit, dragging his tongue to my leaking hole. He circles it with his tongue, torturing me a little before he thrusts his thick, fat tongue inside my virgin hole.

"Oh my god…" My pussy has never been so stuffed before. No one has ever tasted this part of me, ever been inside me like he has. The walls of my pussy pulse around his thick tongue, enjoying the feeling of having something to grab onto.

"You're soaking my tongue in your juices, baby girl," he groans. "Your slutty little pussy is so eager, she's grabbing me hard."

My older tutor sucks and licks my pussy, slurping the juices that leak out of my hole. He fills me up with his tongue again and again, thrusting in and out of my helpless little cunt.

I struggle to breathe, the assault of his tongue on my cunt unbearable. Pleasure skyrockets inside me, pushing me to the edge. My whole body quivers as he thrusts in deeper, his tongue brushing my G-spot for a blessed moment. My cries fill the air. It feels so good to play with my tips while my sexy tutor's mouth latches onto my pussy, sucking and slurping.

"Are you ready to come, baby?" Ronan grabs my hips and squeezes them, letting my hips move in rhythm to his artful fucking. His tongue delves in deeper, finding my sweet spot and licking it.

There's no stopping the climax that gushes over me like a tidal wave. My pussy spasms around his tongue, pulsing with pleasure as I explode into a climax. White light rains down on me, taking me to heaven. I've made myself come before, but nothing has ever come close to his. My fingers grip Ronan's scalp hard, pulling at his hair as he makes me surrender to the ultimate ecstasy. His mouth is greedy and relentless, not stopping even when I'm breaking into a million pieces.

My walls spasm around Ronan's tongue, grabbing him while he fucks me harder with his mouth, tasting my pussy. His lips are sealed over my intimate lips, his tongue filling up my empty hole and curving to intensify my pleasure. The wet sounds he makes when he French kisses my cunt are so damn hot. He won't let me stop, won't let me stop coming until I'm all spent and drained. My pussy purges juices, drenching his tongue in the proof of my pleasure.

It takes me a few minutes to come down from that exuberant high. My nipples are red and sore and swollen and I'm panting like a dog when my eyes finally flicker open. I gaze down my naked body at Ronan's head buried between my thighs. He raises his head, his dark brown eyes gazing at me from between my rising and falling breasts. His lips are glistening with my juices. He licks it and I feel my pussy quiver when he swallows it all up, his big Adam's Apple bobbing up and down. His hair is mussed, his eyes dark and bright, his collared shirt slightly ceased, and he looks good enough to eat.

Ronan emerges from between my legs, collapsing on the bed next to me. Immediately I settle into his arms and he hugs me, holding me close. He's so affected by making me come. I notice his cock is still hard, but he doesn't do anything about it. We breathe unevenly as his hands run all over my back, touching my scars.

"Feeling better?" he asks, planting a kiss on my hair. His muscular arm flexes around my waist, and my pussy flutters at his hotness. Though he's fully clothed, he's the hottest man I've ever seen.

"Better than I've ever felt." I smile, my body buzzing from the orgasm he gave me. "I always felt alone when mom went into one of her moods. I'm glad I stayed with you today, though." I raise my head, kissing Ronan's jaw tentatively. He squeezes my ass in response. "I feel less lonely with you..." My fingers skim lower, touching his flat stomach through his shirt before finding his hard-on. I gently cup this bulge and massage it through his slacks. Ronan moans in response. "You need relief."

My heart flutters because he's put my pleasure first, ignoring his own. He must be aching for relief, but he made me come instead.

"I'll deal with it later." His hand covers mine as his eyes gaze into my baby blues. "Next time someone hurts you, you call me, understand? I'll be here whenever you need me."

His words are messing with my heart, making me want something permanent with him. As I lie naked in bed with my tutor, I don't feel lonely or invisible anymore. I feel safe.

The sounds outside my room have died down. My mom has calmed down by my heart is beating at a million beats per second. The sound of staff moving outside my door wakes me up. Ronan lets me go and rolls off the bed, fishing for my clothes on the floor. I sit up in bed, his scent all over me. Ronan gathers my clothing and places it next to me.

"You're so sexy when you're naked, Elsie. I can't believe I'm the only man who gets to see you like this."

He gazes down at me and then, he leans over and kisses me. My words disappear as his cum-coated lips kiss me hard like they're looking for absolution in me. I kiss him back, enjoying being spoiled by him like this. I can't believe my sexy, uptight tutor actually ate me out after years of yearning. I close my eyes, losing myself in him and he touches my bare stomach, his finger fluttering over its flat surface. Then, he pulls away, his chest rising and falling.

"You're so addictive, baby. I will remember the taste of your cum raining on my tongue all week. Hell, I want to drink from that pussy every day." I blush, feeling reassured that he still desires me. "I don't know how to stop wanting you."

His eyes are lost, sincere and it makes my heart beat a little faster. "Then, don't. I don't ever want to stop wanting you."

"It's not that easy." His lips brush my temple.

The sounds downstairs grow louder and I'm worried my mom is coming upstairs. I roll off the bed, gather my clothes, and put them on. Ronan hurriedly adjusts his collar and shirt, raking his hand through his hair to smooth it down. Then, he helps me with my skirt while I brush my hair. My swollen lips and the scent of sex lingering in the air give me away, but I don't care. When we're fully dressed, Ronan pulls me close, his hands on my hips. We linger like that, him gazing into my eyes and me wanting him to stay, for several moments. Being touched by him has opened the floodgates. I lean into his strong, sturdy body, letting him touch me and hold me. It takes a while for our breaths to calm down, and for our bodies to return to normal. Slowly, Ronan lets me go, moving to the table to gather his books and bag. He walks to the door, watching me all the way.

"Good night. I'll see you next week."

And then, he's gone. The door opens and closes and I'm left alone in my room, my heart filled with big feelings I can't wrap my head around.

CHAPTER 3
RONAN

With my head in my hands, I sit in front of my computer, watching Elsie's empty bedroom. The cameras are working as usual, and next to the video, there's a saved file on my desktop named 'Elsie'. It's the video of me eating her out on her bed. I've jacked off to that video several times since it was filmed. Every night, I dream of her, needing her by my side, needing Elsie's soft body in my bed. It's been almost a week since I ate her pussy in her bedroom, and I've been shaken ever since. My obsession with her has increased tenfold since she told me her parents are trying to get her married.

I breathe jaggedly at the empty room, remembering how I ate her pussy like a starved beast that night. I lost control. One moment I was licking than delicious pussy hoping to take away her pain, and the next, I was making her come on my tongue, lapping up every drop of moisture like it would be my last. The taste of that sweet pussy lingers on my tongue, making me want to take her body again. When she begged me to take her virginity, I wanted to do it. I wanted to sink my cock between those jiggling ass cheeks and stretch that pretty pink pussy. But, I walked home with a hard dick instead and jacked off in the shower. Elsie makes me lose control because I'm so obsessed with her. I never thought revenge would be so hard, but she's making me rethink everything. When I mentioned breeding and her eyes glowed, I wanted to carry her over my shoulder like a caveman and fuck her until she got knocked up. I wanted to wife her up so bad, wanted to give her my last name and make her my little sex toy for life.

Opening another tab, I look at my bank account which shows me six figures in savings. Thanks to my mom's support and my full scholarship, I've saved up a lot of money and even invested in some good stocks. I've been doing a bunch of part-time jobs too, investing that money in new businesses that are starting to pay off. But it's nowhere near enough to keep Elsie in luxury for the rest of our lives. She's a goddess who deserves only the best and despite my growing feelings, I wonder if I can give her that. Sure, I'll get a job after I graduate in a few months, and that would help, but is it enough? I want to take care of her. She's not safe in that house anymore and I want to drag her away from it, into my arms. But she doesn't know that I'm a stalker. She's not safe with me. I'm only using her to get revenge.

A movement on the video screen catches my eye. Elsie walks in wearing a pink halter-neck dress and a shrug to cover her back scars. The deep V-neck of the dress exposes a hint of cleavage, molding to her perky breasts that I sucked last week. Her nipples are hard and pointed, the fabric molding over them to expose her secrets. My nostrils flare when I realize that she's not wearing a bra. Her blonde hair is curled at the ends, making her look like a doll. Elsie raises her doll face to the camera, not knowing that I'm watching her, and pouts with those plump lips lined with gloss. Her big blue eyes are lined with mascara and her petite body trembles in the dress. With one fluid move, Elsie wiggles the shrug off her shoulders, letting it fall to the floor. The deep back of the gown ends right over her hip, showing off her scars. I wonder why she chose to wear that gown.

My little dove moves over to the desk, pulling out a math book of all things. Then, she proceeds to sit on her bed and slowly rolls her gown up. Her flawless calves, knees, and thighs come into view and before I know it she's slipping her fingers between her thighs, touching herself where I kissed her.

"Damn." My cock jumps in response when she begins to stroke herself. Her head falls back, and her eyes shut as she trails her fingers over her slick folds. I can't see her pussy, but I'm dying to.

"Ronan..." My mouth drops from her lips, making my body hot. She adjusts her butt and I know she's wet right now. The dress is tight around her hips and it doesn't stretch, so she slides lower on her bed to give herself more access. "Yes, Daddy. Touch me like that."

Daddy.

Damn, this girl's gonna slay me.

Elsie's head tilts to the right, exposing her shoulder and neck. I want to kiss her there and suck her sensitive skin to leave a love bite. I take a deep breath in, trying to calm myself when the door bursts open.

Elsie immediately closes her thighs, pulling her hand out, but it's too late.

A shadow enters the room and soon, stalking closer to her. Her legs are open, her skirt riding up her thigh. Her shoulders are exposed, and her chest heaves up and down with every breath.

"Bill? What're you doing here?" Her voice erupts just as I catch sight of a preppy college student entering the room. I remember she told me that her parents were trying to get her married to him. Bill looks like a typical spoilt, rich brat in his navy jacket, a pair of matching pants, and a light blue dress shirt. His eyes are fixed on Elsie. She tries to roll off the bed, but he gets there first, using his hand to push her back on the bed. Elsie falls down, her head hitting the pillow, her body exposed to him.

My fist tightens, possessiveness pumping through my veins.

"Your mom said we should get to know each other." He climbs on top of her and her eyes widen in shock.

"Get off me." She tries to push him away, but he doesn't budge. Instead, he grabs her flailing hands and pushes them over her face, making her twist and wriggle.

"You're a naughty little slut, aren't you? You ran away from dinner so that you could get yourself off. George told me you like it when men give you attention." He pokes his index finger out, bringing it to her chest and sliding it down her cleavage."Well, at least that part of our marriage will be satisfactory."

Bill's horse-faced grin lights up the camera and I want to murder him for touching my girl. I shoot out of my seat, grabbing my jacket.

"Stop, please. I don't want you to touch me." Elsie's voice is desperate, her eyes filling with fear.

"Why don't we get to know each other better, huh?" Bill trails his finger around one aroused nipple. "You're not even wearing a bra because you want me so bad. We should get to know each other intimately before the night ends."

"No!"

That's it. I shoot out of my room like a bullet, taking the stairs two steps at a time. There's nothing in my head except the need to rescue Elsie. I sit in my car and take off so fast, swerving and threading through the traffic like a madman. Blood pounds in my head, bile rising in my throat at the thought of Bill touching her, of taking her virginity before I can get to her. I drive like crazy, making the journey between my dorm and her house in under ten minutes. When I park outside the Milligan's mansion, I see something frothy and pink moving in the dark. I rush out of my car, running to the front gate in record time just to see Elsie bursting out of it. She runs straight into my arms, her panicked eyes looking back as she runs barefoot. Her body collides with my chest and I wrap my big arms around her, holding her close. Her panicked eyes shoot up and when she sees me, she calms down a little.

"Ronan?" She's only wearing her gown, breathing unevenly as tears fill her eyes. "You're really here?"

She looks shaken like she's running from Bill. She must've run away from him when he tried to have his way with her. Other than her disheveled hair, she looks fine. Thank god, she's safe.

"I'm here, baby," I hold her tight, letting her settle her head on my chest. I kiss her head, hugging her to restore a sense of safety. She's clearly shaken because that bastard tried to put his hands on her without permission. "You're safe now."

"Bill...he..." Tears erupt from her eyes and my heart breaks. I swipe her salty tears with my thumb kissing her temple.

"It's okay, Elsie. I'm here now. Nobody can hurt you, baby girl." Her small hands tighten around my waist, her entire body shaking.

"Ronan..." She manages to squeeze my name out between sobs. Her glassy blue eyes meet mine. "Please, take me away."

―――

Elsie stands in my dorm room minutes later, wearing my jacket. After I found her barefoot outside her house, I brought her here. She's a pop of pink in my dreary black dorm room. I don't share the room with anyone and my flatmate, who has the other room, is traveling this weekend, making us the only two people in the house. My laptop is closed, my bedsheets folded, and I wish I had more time to fix this place before I brought her here.

"So, this is what a Harvard dorm looks like." She takes in the fan on the floor, leaning her ass against my desk. It isn't too warm as fall is beckoning. "This might be the closest I ever get to it." She smiles and I feel relieved seeing she's back to her usual self. When I saw her crying, I almost lost it. I wanted to tear Bill from limb to limb with my bare hands and bury him in the backyard for daring to touch my girl.

Mine. She's mine. Every cell in my body knows it.

"It's a little small…basic." She shrugs and I love how she looks in my jacket. It's too big for her, but she looks mine.

"It's functional," I admit, trying not to startle her with my concern. I hover a few inches from her, breathing roughly. We both don't address the elephant in the room—what happened a few moments ago. She doesn't ask me how I knew when to come and I don't tell her. Instead, I admire her profile as she turns, taking in the pictures on my wall. Her finger skims over a picture of my brother. She touches the Polaroid, making my heart jump.

"Who is this? He looks a lot like you."

"My brother," I confess.

"You have a brother? I thought you were the only kid. I guess I don't know much about you." She gazes at the other pictures of mom with us, of mom and me, and of my brother and me. "Is he older?" she asks, turning to me, and I nod. "Is he studying here too? He looks really smart with those spectacles."

"He was." She waits for me to finish that sentence, but I don't. Instead, I take another step forward, feeling the blazing attraction between us. It feels forbidden to have her here, touching the laptop I use to stalk her, seeing photos of my brother who her brother bullied. It reminds me of our complicated relationship.

"Where's he now?" She wants to know more about me, and I want her to give this tonight.

"He died." Elsie blinks.

"I'm sorry. I didn't know…" Elsie turns back and I take one more step until my knees are brushing her thigh. She's a good head shorter than me, her body tiny in comparison to mine, but her light fills up the darkness in my soul.

"He would've liked you." My hand shoots out, grabbing the desk for support. My move cages Elsie who puts her hand over my white knuckles. Her palm slides up my cheek, cupping my jaw on one side. She's too close, slipping through my cracks like water.

"Yeah?" Her voice is soft and tentative. She has eyes only for me and I love it. This moment between us seems more intimate than any sex. It's like she's looking deep into my soul while she tries to bare hers to me.

I nod. "You're easy to like, Elsie." Our eyes meet and a shiver passes through her body. I watch her nipples pucker under the tight pink bodice of her dress, getting hard just for me. She's dancing with the devil and she doesn't even know it.

"Your brother…he must've been really young. How did he die?" She's curious about me. Elsie wants to comfort me the way I comfort her, but she has no idea how twisted I am.

I want to lie to her and say it was an accident, but I can't. "He killed himself." Her eyes widen. "He was as old as you when I…" I shut my eyes, my fingers fisting. Her fingers touch my hard knuckle, giving me comfort. "He was being bullied…some rich kid was threatening him. My brother tried to fight it, but he spread lies around school and—" My voice breaks.

"Ronan." Elsie moves closer, her soft fingers on my cheek keeping me alive.

"I wish I knew before. Mom and I were in the dark. He couldn't even speak to us about it." I close my eyes, pressing

MY TUTOR, MY STALKER 37

my forehead to Elsie's. "When I found him dead in his room…I was devastated. We had planned to go to college together. Suddenly, he was gone and I was alone."

Elsie quietly listens to my story. I've never told anyone this before, never broken down in front of a girl like this. The ugly memories of that fateful day wash over me, pulling me under. I fight the currents like I've been doing for so many years, struggling to stay above the water.

"What about the boy who bullied him? Did they ever punish him?" Her sweet voice is the only thing that makes me want to go on.

"No. He got away with it. There was no proof even though every kid in my brother's class knew what was going on. They couldn't speak out against him or his Dad would ruin them. Imagine losing your brother and not even being able to get justice for what he went through." My breathing is rough. I gaze into my baby girl's eyes, seeing nothing but sympathy in them.

Her thumb brushes over my cheek, her eyes all for me. "I can't believe you've been carrying this burden all on your own. And I thought you were uptight. I'm sorry. I had no idea."

"It's not your fault," I tell her. "You are the brightest thing in my life. Seeing you every weekend makes me feel better." I grab her waist and pull her closer, my lips lightly brushing over hers. We're both desperate for physical contact, and the touch of my lips makes her moan. "And we aren't here to talk about me. What happened tonight, Elsie?" She's aroused, her eyes closed and her eyelashes fluttering open and close when my lips brush hers. "Why did you run away?"

"I…" She opens her eyes, gazing at me. "Bill came onto me. I said no, but he wouldn't stop. I kicked him off and ran away." Her body shakes as she recounts the episode. My thumb smooths over her shoulder, trying to calm her down. "I don't know what I'd have done if you weren't there. I have nowhere else to go." Her eyes are glassy when she looks up. I hate that he made her look like this.

"You'll always have me, little dove." I press a soft, slow kiss to her lips. "You know that you can always come to me. I'll protect you."

She nods. "Ronan…I…" Her eyelashes lower, touching her cheek. "I don't want to go back home. Please, let me stay here with you tonight." She's clinging to me like a child and I want to keep her safe. "I don't want anyone but you. When he touched me, I just knew that it was wrong. I only want to be yours. I want you to be the only man who touches me, who kisses me, who sees me naked, and makes me come. I want to scream your name when I come, wake up next to you with your cum inside me, and fall asleep in your arms." Her words are making me hot, and needy for the inevitable.

"I'll never let you go, baby. You're mine now." My words are a possessive grunt. "Your body, your soul, your pussy, it all belongs to me." Elsie nods, choking on emotion.

"Yes, Daddy."

God, that word makes me come undone. I silence her lips with a burning kiss, sealing her mouth with mine. Elsie's moans die, her stomach rubbing on my bulge as she surrenders to me. Her body slumps while I hold her. Pushing my jacket off her shoulder, I touch her bare back, reacclimatizing myself with her scars. I love touching them, love reassuring her that I love her just as she is. The mating of our mouths is an inferno, making my cock hard as a rock. I kiss her hard, holding her body like she's precious to me. Her palms frame my face, letting me drink her in like oxygen. I kiss my baby girl like a starved man who needs her love to survive. My hands run all over her body, touching her everywhere through that tempting pink dress. When her hands drop, her fingers fluttering over my erection, I jerk my hips violently against her palm.

Tearing my mouth from hers, I command, "Get on your knees, Elsie."

My words are rough, making her eyes widen with lust. But Elsie is obedient. She drops to her knees, her gown stretching around her flared hips. When she gazes up from between my legs, her breasts hanging like teardrops, I lose it. I undo my belt and buttons, letting my jeans drop to the floor. I'm not wearing any underwear because I was watching her, knowing I'd want to touch myself when the object of my obsession entered the screen.

Her eyes pop wide open when she catches the first glimpse of my massive cock, veined and throbbing. Pre-cum leaks out of my swollen tip and she licks those juicy, gloss-lined pink lips in response.

"Touch me, baby," I growl. "I've been dreaming of having those plump lips wrapped around my cock for months."

She tentatively brings her hand to my throbbing member, grabbing me with other palms. The touch of her cool, soft palm against my sensitive, velvety skin is a revelation. My balls tighten in response. "You're so big." She breaths unevenly, sliding her hand up and down my bare shaft, feeling the veins throb under her. "I've never seen anything like it...."

"Touch me how you want, Elsie. What do you want to do to my cock, baby?"

She gazes up at me with those big, blue eyes before turning back down. Elsie brings her thumb to my tip, spreading the pre-cum around my head with slow, deliberate motions. My core clenches, heat flooding my veins as she spreads my pre-cum all over my shaft, lubricating it. "Am I doing it right?"

"Damn right." My voice is a growl as she moves her fist up and down my length, pausing when she reaches my thick root, Her knuckles brush against my balls, making my lust roar to life. I can't go slow with her, I need her too much. "Put your mouth where you put your thumb, baby. Swallow my dick like you want."

Her fingers stop and I hear a sharp intake of breath. She wants to suck dick. I can feel it. Slowly, she lowers her hands and brings her mouth forward. The first touch of those plump, pink lips to my tip sends me to heaven.

"Fuck, Elsie, you were born for this." She smiles, opening her mouth and taking my tip between her fat lips. Electricity zips through my spine as her mouth closes around my most sensitive crown, her tongue licking circles around my tip. I lean forward and grab her hair violently, pulling at it as she tortures me with that wet tongue of hers. "Baby, you're too good at this. Take me deeper."

With a moan that vibrates along my length, she begins swallowing me. My cock slides between her lips, disappearing deeper with every stroke. I move my hips pushing into her as her fingers come up to touch and tease my balls. She cups and gently massages them as my need blazes out of control. I thrust hard into her mouth, filling her up. Her mouth to too small to take my entire cock and she cries out when my tip hits the back of her throat.

"Deeper, baby. I want you to choke on Daddy's cock." I massage her scalp, trying to relax her. "Take a deep breath and relax." She follows my instructions, breathing while I wait for her to adjust to the intrusion. Then, I push in deeper, squeezing through the back of her throat until she's gagging. Mascara tears leak from her eyes, marring her pretty face, but she takes my cock all the way until her lips are stretched over my girthy root.

"Good girl." I pat her head. She looks up from between my legs, waiting for the next instructions. Her fingers on my balls are killing me, but she doesn't stop. "Now it's time to suck."

Without warning, I begin thrusting in and out of her mouth. Elsie whimpers when I draw my cock back and thrust it between her lips, making her body shake. My balls slap her face, my cock swelling in her mouth. Her throat works as she sucks me, licking the underside of my shaft and the throbbing veins. She times her sucks with my thrusts, blowing me when I pound into her. My hips violently rock into my girl's mouth, destroying those pretty little lips. I fill her up with my big dick, again and again, an orgasm building when she sucks my cock like a baby. My thrusts grow fast and furious, going so deep that I leave a scar at the back of her throat. She gags when I choke her with my dick, making her eyes water. My dick slides in and out of her sexy mouth, her lipgloss coating my shaft. Every breath burns my lungs. My orgasm balloons, threatening to spill any moment.

"I'm so close to coming…" I rasp. Elsie takes my cock like a good cum dump, letting me go hard as she grabs my thighs and sucks hard on my cock. Pleasure spears through my center, making me see stars. "Just like that, little dove. Suck me like that when I'm spraying cum down your throat."

I push her limits, thrusting deeper and she never stops sucking, even as she's flickering in and out of consciousness. I fuck her mouth hard, my balls smacking her face until there's no controlling my climax. Elsie makes me come with one final suck, her sweet voice moaning around my dick.

My body breaks apart, the flames of my climax engulfing me. I see nothing but darkness as my orgasm pulls me under, making every cell in my body light up with bliss. My balls explode, spitting cum into Elsie's virgin mouth. With wet moans, she swallows every single drop, her eager sounds making me come even harder. She loves being my little dick sucker, taking her Daddy's cock like it's the greatest privilege in the world.

She wasn't kidding when she said she liked sucking because she blows me like a champ. Her mouth never stops moving, hungrily lapping up my cum like a greedy slut. She enjoys the taste of my salty shaft and my cum, drinking it like water. I keep coming and coming inside her until my legs are shaky. Elsie matches me thrust for thrust, her eagerness a perfect complement to my passion. My cum fills her mouth until it's dripping down her swollen lips, onto that expensive dress.

I breathe hard, trying to gather myself when my cock goes soft inside her mouth. I'm spent and drained, pleasure filling me up. Damn, I've wanted this for so long that it feels unreal.

I let go of Elsie's blonde hair reluctantly, slowly pulling my cock out from between her lips. She gazes up at me, her lips bruised and swollen from all that cock sucking. She's been such a good girl and I want to reward her pussy by stretching it tonight. Her doll face is the most beautiful thing in the world, especially when she's on her knees.

"Get up, baby." I pull my shirt over my head, leaving me completely naked. Elsie gets to her feet shakily and I pull her back onto the bed with me. I lay her out on the sheets, kissing her cum-stained lips and moaning when I taste myself on them. Her swollen lips part for me, marked with my release. "You did so good, little dove. You need to be rewarded for sucking my dick so good."

"Really?" she asks, her hands falling to her sides when I caress her cheeks. My lips trail lower, kissing her neck as she moans in my bed. I find the sweet spot at the base of her neck and suckle, making her pussy clench in response.

"Ronan..."

"You like it when I do that?" I ask, adding my teeth to the assault. Raising one hand, I cup her tit and squeeze it lightly. My thumb teases her beaded nipple, rubbing it through the fabric.

"Mmmm...I like everything you do to me." She arches into my touch, letting me cup her entire tit while I kiss and suck on her neck.

"You're so darn tempting, Elsie. I don't even know how I lived so long without you." I suck extra hard and she screams when her neck bruises with my mark. I lick it, kissing the spot I claimed.

"Me too. I need you all the time, Ronan. I've never felt like this before." Her body is hot and responsive to my touches and there's no denying what we both want.

"I'm going to make your wish come true tonight, baby." I raise my head, watching her expression transform. "I'm going to stretch that ripe little cunt and make you mine."

CHAPTER 4
ELSIE

Ronan looms over me, his words echoing in my ears.

I'm going to make you mine.

His gray eyes are blazing with hunger, making my pussy steadily drip for my older tutor. A strand of dark, sweaty hair sticks to his temple, and my body buzzes with anticipation for my tutor. He's the stalker and I'm the prey, and I want him to hunt me down. My body throbs for him, my pussy tingling from sucking his dick. My lips are swollen after taking my tutor's big cock, but I want more. I want him to put it inside me and make me a woman.

"Tell me you want this, Elsie." His thumb rubs my lower lip.

I'm wetter than an ocean, my womb pulsing needily for my man. Since the moment he took me away from my house, I knew this would happen. When I heard the story about his brother my heart broke. Ronan isn't just hot, he's deep and I want to share his burdens a little. We're more alike than I thought, both of us finding sanctuary in each other.

When he showed up at my door to rescue me like a knight in shining armor, I knew he was the one. Despite his grumpiness, he's always looking out for me, protecting me like no one ever has. When he came in my mouth, I could taste his desire for me, and I knew I wanted this man to be my first, my last, my everything. With him by my side, I have hope for a better life, one filled with love and happiness.

"I want this," I whisper. "I want you, Ronan. I want you to pop my cherry and make me bleed for you. Please, Daddy, make me yours. I never want to know any dick but yours."

"Fuck, baby. You're so good for me." He kisses my bruised lips. "I want to worship your body all night.' His hands reach for the ribbon tying my halter neck up. With one tug, he loosens the ribbon loosening the tie holding my top together. As it falls, he grabs it and pulls it down, revealing my bra-less tits, my nipples hard enough to cut glass.

"You're so horny, little dove." He rolls his tongue over my aroused nipple and I whimper. His calloused thumb teases my other hard tip, rubbing over it. Sparks shoot down my core, and I rub my thighs together in a desperate attempt to stop myself from coming. "Have you been dreaming of me sucking those titties since that night?"

"Yes...." His hand reaches under my dress, pulling it up so that it bunches over my knee. Ronan kisses my breasts, flicking one nipple with his tongue and making it harder. My fingers dig into his hair, loving the way he possesses me. I can feel him getting harder when he swallows my nipple and suckles on it, making my body flip inside out. His one suck makes my insides blaze with need. My toes curl when he pinches my other nipple, using my body for his pleasure.

I arch my back, giving him access to the zipper at the back. He grabs it, dragging it down my ass to undo the gown. "I've been wanting to take this gown off ever since I saw it. What were you doing having dinner with Bill without a bra? I could see those hard nipples from miles away." He bites on one tip and I cry out. "These perfect titties are for my gaze only, do you understand?"

"Yes...." He swirls his tongue around my tip, teasing my

helpless nipple until it's hard and aroused, my clit throbbing. He drags my dress over my knees and pushes it to the floor.

"Open your legs. Let me see how wet sucking my dick made you." I open my legs on command, my skin tightening with pleasure when he drags a thick finger over my soaked folds. "Damn, your pussy is creaming, baby girl. It's so ready to take my cock."

His man meat presses against my thigh as he kisses my body, trailing kisses all over my tits, lightly licking the underside of my breast before he places a kiss on my belly button. My stomach quivers and when he kisses me there again, I grab his hair, imagining him kissing me like this when I'm swollen with his seed. Ever since he promised to breed me, I've been having dreams about getting pregnant with Ronan's baby.

"I want to make this flat belly swell with my seed." He reads my thoughts. "I wanna kiss you again and again when you're big and swollen with our child, knowing I put that baby inside you." His dick hardens against my skin and I feel his pre-cum leaking onto my thigh. "The need to possess you is primal, Elsie." He squeezes my hip with his fingers. "It's like you were meant to be mine...my sexy little housewife who will be waiting for her man with her big belly when he comes home from work. I'd flip that tiny skirt of yours up and sink my dick into your wet, needy pussy in the living room with all the neighbors watching. They'd hear your scream when you come for me."

My pussy contracts, his dirty words weaving a spell. I want this dream to be real so bad. I thought I was too young to get married, but being Ronan's wife feels so natural like it is what I was born to do. Images of welcoming my hardworking man home, carrying his babies, and falling asleep in his arms flood my brain until my body is begging for him.

His fingers touch my clit, rubbing my hard little pearl. "I'd suck on your clit until you came, baby." He pulls my bead between two fingers rolling it around.

"Aaahhh…."

"I'd call you by my last name." His words are rougher, more possessive. "And I'd make sure my woman was always well-pleasured." He pulls and tugs at my clit and I am breaking open.

"Ronan…I need you." Ronan loosens his grip on my clit, letting it go with one final pinch. I look down and see that he's all hard and aroused again, his thick cock ready to pop my cherry. Licking my lips, I gaze into his eyes, teetering on the precipice of this special moment. "Breed me, Daddy. Make me a Mommy. I want to carry your baby in my womb."

I don't care about the future. All that matters at this moment with Ronan. I want him to give me a gift, to put a baby inside me so that I can always carry a part of him.

"Damn, how can I refuse you, baby? Hearing you say those words makes me want to knock you up right now." He emits a feral growl, gripping his cock and running his fat head all over my slippery seam. Sparks erupt everywhere.

"It feels so good." He runs his tip up and down my length, lubricating me for our lovemaking. "You feel so good."

"If it hurts, you tell me," he rasps, watching me, as his tip circles my slippery hole. I nod.

Ronan sinks the fat tip of his cock into my cunt, stretching me as he penetrates me for the first time. My entire body clenches up, feeling the invasion everywhere.

"Easy, baby. Just follow my lead." He kisses my mouth, rolling my nipples with his fingers as he slides deeper into me. My fleshy walls expand to accommodate his girth. Every inch that he sinks into my hot sex is like an explosion in my mind.

"Fuck, you're so tight, Elsie, choking my cock with that virgin pussy." Ronan's cock is so big, the delicious stretch making me lose my mind for a moment. When Ronan pushes another inch, I feel something tear.

"Ronan...." My nails sink into his biceps when he pops my cherry. A stinging ache travels through my core, my maidenhead gone. Ronan pauses, giving me time to adjust. He kisses me all over my face, and I know he's doing it to make me feel better.

"I'm here, baby. Look at me. I'm going to make you feel good." His eyes are fixed on me as he slowly pushes his cock deeper into my pussy, stretching me to the max. As he sinks deeper, my body adjusts to his size, the pain transforming into curiosity. "Let me into that tight little pussy, little dove. Let me breed that ripe cunt so good you'll be begging for more." He keeps going until his fat cock is ensconced between my silky folds, filling me up. My pussy lips hug his thick root, his balls resting against my ass. He gently rubs my stomach, kissing my mouth. "Good girl. You look so good stuffed with my cock." The sensation of being filled with his length is new and unfamiliar but my body grows accustomed to it with every passing moment. He stays inside me for a moment, letting me adjust to the invasion.

Then, he begins to move. Grabbing my hips, he fucks me in slow, shallow strokes, creating a pleasant vibration inside my core. "God, the thought of you coming all over my cock, drenching me with your virgin blood and cum makes me want to come inside you right now." I whimper, pleasure building with every little stroke. The neediness is back with a vengeance, my pussy walls clutching his cock in a desperate plea for more. "Are you ready to be railed by my cock, baby?"

"Yes...." I surrender control of my body to Ronan who begins moving deeper. He pulls his cock almost all the way out and slams into my tender little hole, making my entire body shake like an earthquake. "Oh my god...." A flash of pleasure blinds me, stealing my breath. Ronan goes harder, drilling my pussy with his wet, fat cock until his balls are slapping against my ass. My body turns into a pool of hot lava, burning bright for only him. He fucks me deep and hard, and I scream when the tip of his cock hits my cervix. I've never taken anyone that deep before.

"God, your tight little pussy is making me lose control. I want to rail you all night, baby." My little pussy slurps my tutor's cock with wet sounds. "I can't wait to feel it clenching around my cock when you come. You're so close, Elsie. I can feel it."

His dirty words are making me see stars. With every claiming thrust, he takes me higher, making my pleasure reach a fever pitch before it shatters. Our joining is hot and sweaty and it feels so good to be railed by him, possessed like I'm the only woman who matters. When his cock scrapes against my G-spot, I unravel like a ball of yarn.

"Ronan!" I scream his name as my entire body goes still, an orgasm taking over. My pussy spasms around my tutor's cock, squeezing his massive dick like an anaconda. Bliss coats my senses, carrying me off to a land of endless pleasure. I've never felt so good before, never felt as ecstatic as I feel when Ronan is inside me, giving me the perfect amount of friction to detonate.

"Fuck, baby, I'm gonna come inside you." He's on his last thread of control and when I squeeze my thighs together, it snaps. Ronan comes inside me with a loud grunt, our sweaty bodies joining together in a double climax. His cock swells inside me and explodes, raining cum all over my inner walls. "Mmmm…baby take my cum into the ripe little pussy and grow my seed in your stomach." His balls spit a heavy load of seed into my unprotected womb, breeding me like he promised. There's so much that it leaks out of my spasming hole, sliding down my ass, but Ronan doesn't stop coming inside me.

His hands touch my naked body everywhere as I cling to

him, continuing to come on his thick cock. It's the best feeling in the world—being plugged up by my hot tutor while he breeds me with his hot seed. The heat trickles inside my belly, making me want to be a mommy so bad.

We keep coming like that for a few moments until we've been wrung out. I open my eyes, panting under my tutor, watching sweat drip down his hair strands. His eyes are dark as he slumps over my naked body. He holds me close, his cock still buried inside me, and kisses my cheek.

"Damn, I've never come that hard before. You're perfect, Elsie." His lips trail down my jaw, pressing a soft kiss on my lips. "Are you feeling all right?"

"I feel really good," I admit. "When you came inside me… I…I loved it."

He smiles. "You're even more addictive than I thought. I want to keep you in bed all night and rail that pussy until you're too sore to walk."

"Who's stopping you?" I ask, feeling naughty as I slide my fingers down his exposed arm. "I'm not going anywhere."

"No, you aren't." His voice is breathy. "But we both need to eat after that intense orgasm. I don't want you fainting at midnight."

He pulls out of me and I purr when I feel the loss of his cock. It emerges from my pussy, all wet and coated in my cum and blood. He grunts at the sight, pulling my hand up and kissing it. "Thank you for giving me your first time, Elsie. Coming inside you is the best feeling, baby."

"I…I enjoyed it too," I admit. "More than I thought I would. The girls said the first time is always painful but you made it so good for me." I touch my belly that's stuffed with his cum. "Maybe breeding is my kink."

He laughs. "I sure hope so because I plan to breed several times before sunrise."

CHAPTER 5
RONAN

Elsie lies on my bare chest, her little fingers making patterns on my exposed stomach. "How do you have abs like that?" she asks, opening her mouth as I feed her a potato chip. "All you eat is junk food."

I laugh, Elsie curled against me. "I hit the gym regularly."

She's so adorable dressed in my oversized t-shirt, relaxing after an intense lovemaking session.

I made some dinner for us after I got her into my shower. We both showered together and I couldn't stop kissing her as she clung to me. She's so beautiful when she's naked, but wearing nothing but my oversized shirt, she looks adorable. Her exposed thighs spread out on my narrow bed, and she rests her face on the crook of my arm. The fact that she isn't wearing anything under that shirt makes me hard. I'm always hard around her.

"I do pilates too but I look nothing like you."

"You look perfect." I kiss her little button nose.

Our empty dinner plates lie on my desk, the sheets smelling of sex. I'm going to save them to remind me of the first time I made love to Elsie. I love feeding her and taking care of her. I never thought it'd be so enjoyable. Elsie opens her sexy mouth and bites off the chip. We've moved on from dinner to snacks. Soon, I'll be feasting on her pussy for dessert.

"Mmmm… this tastes so good. Mom doesn't let me eat junk food. She says I'll get fat and then men will lose interest in me." I push another potato chip between her lips which are still wet and swollen from sucking her tutor's massive dick. My cum sloshing inside her unprotected womb, she's all mine in this moment.

"Bullshit. You're the most beautiful woman in the world and putting on weight will only make you even more beautiful." I put my arm around her waist and pull her close. My lips descend on hers, kissing her possessively to prove my point. "I'm never going to lose interest in you, especially once you become a sexy Momma and put on weight."

When I say those words, they sound real. Far too real. I'm in deep for this girl, and sitting in my room, eating with her, and making love doesn't feel like revenge. No, it feels like something I'd want to do for the rest of my life. A mixture of fear and knowing echoes in my heart. I thought I could just breed her and forget about her, but Elsie is more than a revenge ploy to me. Holding her close reminds me that she's someone I care about.

"Mmm…" Her eyes flutter open and closed, but her mouth curves down in a frown. Looking away, she says, "Every time you say that, I wish it could be real."

"What?"

"Me becoming the mother of your kids, living with you, being yours." Her bright blue eyes hit me, making my heart pulse. "I think…I'd love that."

"Yeah?" How did we go from potato chips to this? I want to reassure her, tell her I'll make her mine no matter what it takes, but I'm lying to her even now. She doesn't know why I became her tutor and if she ever finds the proof of my stalking, she'd be scared of me.

"Yeah." I caress her blonde hair. "I'd love to be your wife…to stay home and wait for my hot husband to get home from work every day and let you make love to me every night. We could just kiss or talk or just linger, kissing each other for hours. I think I'd even enjoy doing mundane things like cooking if it was with you."

"You like me that much?" I tease.

She blushes before giving a little nod. "All I've known is a life of material luxury and emotional insecurity. Sometimes, I wish I were born a normal person. I could fall in love, get married, and have a family like regular people do without worrying about family connections."

"I might not be able to provide everything your father does," I remind myself. "I've still got a few months to graduate and while I plan to get a job, even a well-paying one, I don't know if it'll be enough."

Her palm rubs my cheek, my stubble abrading her soft hands. "I don't care. What matters is that I feel safe and loved with you. That's worth more than money. I wouldn't regret choosing happiness. Nobody does."

She's such a pure soul. I don't know many girls who'd want to give up a life of material comfort just to be with someone they love.

I hold up another chip, tugging at her lip. "In that case, eat all you want. I love feeding you, and we've both established I'd be obsessed with you even if you gained weight." She eats the chip, licking her lips.

"You're so nice to me. I wish I could just stay here with you forever." Her phone pings and she ignores it.

"Who's that?" I ask, reaching for her phone.

"Dad. He's been texting me about what a mess I made during the dinner. I told him I'm at a friend's and won't be back until tomorrow." The light in Elsie's eyes disappears a little as she rests her head on my chest. "They're angry."

I take her phone and turn it off, cutting off her Dad's

messages. The thought of sending Elsie back to that abusive home where her parents could hurt her is unbearable. However, that was my original plan. I don't know what to make of my feelings for her.

"Look at me, baby. You're here with me now and that's all that matters. No one can hurt you now and I'm sure as hell not letting you go until your parents have calmed down. For tonight, only think about the pleasure I'm going to give you."

I put the bag of chips on the desk and push Elsie down. Her shirt skids up, exposing that ripe little pussy that's already wet for me. She looks at me, trust filling her blue eyes as I drag her shirt up and over her head. When she's naked, I take off my pants and release my cock. Elsie holds it in her little hands, palming and stroking me until I'm dripping pre-cum onto her belly.

When I'm hard and ready, I bury myself inside her, this time, without any warning. She's ready for me, melting under me the moment I start moving inside her. I suck on her swollen nipples and leave whisker burns all over her skin as I rail her hard and come inside her for the second time in one night. We collapse on each other, catching our breath before going for another round.

By the time the first rays of the sun break through, her pussy is destroyed and I've pumped her with enough cum to have a dozen kids. Elsie lays on my arm, both of us sweaty on my bed, as I shut my eyes, trying to get some sleep before it's time for classes.

When my eyes close, I hear Elsie whisper in my ear, "I love you."

Instantly, my heart stills, but I don't open my eyes. Her fingers draw patterns on my chest, her body nestled close to me. He kisses my mouth. "I love you."

MY TUTOR, MY STALKER 55

Two weeks later —

My phone pings with a message in the morning, and I slow down the treadmill I'm working out on. The university gym is crowded during the weekend, and while I work out, I remember how much Elsie loves my abs. I'm going to keep working on them for her.

It's been two weeks since I first made love to Elsie and we've been texting ever since. After that first night together, I dropped her home, making sure her parents didn't see me. I knew they wouldn't be happy at the prospect of Elsie having spent the night with her tutor, but as I watched her go, my heart was in pain.

I heard what she said that night as we fell asleep.

I love you.

The words play in an endless loop in my mind as I glance down at my phone.

Elsie: Mom and Dad are going out tonight. We can have fun when you come to tutor me.

After I came inside Elsie all night, she was sore for an entire week. I got some medication delivered to her house so that she could feel better, and they worked, because a week later when I came in for our weekly tutoring session, she was excited and healed, begging me to fuck her again. Since I couldn't do it with her mom downstairs, I settled for eating her pussy. She sucked me off afterward, saying she wanted to meet up in my dorm again. I snuck her a bag of potato chips that she saved in her secret stash but as I kissed her goodbye, I knew a week away from her would be hell.

I watch her every day, but that's no longer enough. I want her next to me. I want to touch her, smell her, taste her, and tell her how much I adore her. I want her in my house, in my life, and as my wife. Ever since she confessed to wanting to be my little housewife, I've been obsessed with marrying her. Marrying her would ruin my plan, but I'm beginning to think the plan doesn't matter anymore. Having her is

Ronan: Sounds good. I'll bring my dick;)
Elsie: OMG, my favorite thing in the world.
Elsie: I can't wait.

Neither can I. Her texts always light me up. I've touched her only twice since that night and I need to be inside her again to feel sane. She's a revelation in bed, so responsive and passionate. We have great chemistry, and though I expected that, I didn't expect how easily I'd get addicted to her sweetness. Away from her controlling family, she's an exuberant woman. I want her light to shine, I want to take her somewhere she can just be herself.

Elsie looked so lonely when she said she wished she could be a normal person. When she said she'd love to be my wife, I wanted to ask her to be mine, but before that, I needed to figure out how to deal with the aftermath.

My phone begins ringing and I realize it's mom calling. I switch off the treadmill and get off, answering the call.

"Mom." I wish I could ask her for advice right now. She's always been on my side.

"How's my boy doing?" she asks. "The finals are just six months away. I can't believe you'll graduate so soon. I've been wondering if I should book my tickets for your graduation."

"You should." My voice is devoid of any emotion as I say it, my mind stuck on Elsie.

"You don't sound that excited. What's wrong? Is my son having girl problems?" She says it in jest, but when I don't reply, Mom adds, "You really have girl problems. I can't believe it."

"Why not?"

"You've never shown interest in any girl." That's because I've been obsessed with Elsie. "I'm so happy you have someone. Tell me more about her."

"She's younger than me," I hazard. I leave out the part

about her being in high school. "And well, her folks are really well off."

"Ah. You think you're not good enough."

"It's not that." I swallow. "I think she could do better than me."

"Even though you love her?"

"How do you know that?" I catch my words, realizing I just confessed to loving Elsie to my mother. God, I'm really fucked now.

"Oh my god, you're in love. It makes me really proud as your mom to know I raised a normal human being." I grunt. "You've been so obsessed with Levi's death ever since he passed away. I was starting to worry you'd spend your entire life trying to make up for that."

"What do you mean?"

"I know you didn't want to study Math at Harvard. You were always interested in numbers, but more from a business perspective than a theoretical one. But after your brother died, you changed. You said you wanted to study Math."

"I do like math."

"But not as much as you like other things. It's what your brother would've wanted. He always wanted to go to Harvard for Math, and I wonder sometimes if you feel guilty because you got to live instead of him. Is that why you're doing things you think he would?" Her insight stuns me.

"I like what I'm doing."

"That's good, but I hope you're not doing it for the wrong reasons. Ronan…I've seen the images in your room. You're far too obsessed with George and your brother's death." She's wrong. "I don't want you to waste your life getting justice for him. Revenge isn't going to bring him back."

"Mom, you knew?"

"I had a hunch. When you started tutoring at the Mulligans', I was worried you were going down that path."

"But… what he did to Levi was unforgivable. If it wasn't for him, my brother would still be alive."

"He's my son too," Mom reminds me. "And I miss him every day. I want to get justice for him too, but not if it means losing my other son." I hear her voice break and worry immediately fills my head. "I want you to be happy, Ronan. It's my job as an adult to get justice for Levi. I don't want you to carry that burden alone. If Levi were really around, he wouldn't want you to spend your life on revenge. He'd want you to be happy, and do the things you've always wanted to do."

"Mom…" My breathing is shaky. I grip the edge of the wall, just outside the shower.

"Be happy, Ronan. Go after that girl you love. That's the best revenge."

A profound realization washes over me and I realize that it's time to go for what I want, despite the odds. Maybe Mom is right. Marrying Elsie might be the best revenge ever.

I shower and then I go check my savings account. It looks like I'm going to be buying a wedding ring.

CHAPTER 6
ELSIE

I tap my foot on the wooden floor, eagerly awaiting Ronan. My window is open and my eyes are fixed on the empty driveway. Ever since I messaged him, I've been aching to see him. It's been two weeks since he came inside me, and every moment since then has been spent in agony, waiting for the next time I can be his. With Mom and Dad in the house, he didn't take me during our tutoring sessions, though he did give me some relief. I considered visiting his university again, but with all the Bill drama, I couldn't sneak away.

Dad was angry when I came back home after my night with Ronan. He didn't ask who I'd spent the night with. Instead, he launched into a plan to win Bill back. My parents spent the entire day berating me for turning away Bill and putting their plans in jeopardy. Thankfully, Mom didn't hit me because Dad was there. George came too, saying I should at least be able to get married to his friend, even if I can't do anything else. He said he'd talk to Bill and try to fix things but I'm not interested in Bill at all.

At first, I thought I could go back to my planned existence once I tasted desire with Ronan, but letting him come unprotected inside me has changed me. I find myself wanting to break the shackles of my current existence more and more. Life only makes sense when I'm with him.

I place my hand over my flat belly, wondering if I'm pregnant already. I have a few exams to go and then, I'll graduate. I always thought I'd want to go to college or travel the world after school, but when Ronan whispered dirty fantasies about making me his pregnant housewife, I knew that was my dream. I want to be with a man I love and create the happy family I never had. In Ronan's arms, I feel safe, and now that I've known his kisses, no other man will ever do.

The sound of a car engine downstairs makes me stand up. Ronan parks his car next to the gate and gets out. The moment I lay eyes on his sexy face, his stubble overgrown, his long, powerful legs clad in tailored black pants, my pussy begins to quiver. He's wearing a white dress shirt, looking all professional. We've got just two more weeks of tutoring to go, and I desperately want to find a reason to keep seeing him.

The doorbell rings, making an excited shiver snake up my spine. I wait in my room quietly, letting the maid open the door for my hot tutor. My heart drums with every step Ronan takes up the staircase, even though I can't hear him. When he knocks on my door, I know it's time. I reach for my golden door handle and twist it, revealing the image of the man I love.

"Good evening, Elsie." His voice is smooth as whisky, his sexy silver eyes watching me. His brown hair is slicked back.

"Good evening, Mr. Jackson."

My pussy quivers when I call him by his last name.

I'd call you by my last name, he said when he made love to me. The thought of being his wife, of carrying his name is making my insides hot. That night, I confessed to loving him after he fell asleep. I've been wondering if I should say those words out loud to him again because my feelings have only become stronger since.

I open the door wider, letting him in. As soon as he's in, he throws his bag to the ground, grabs my waist, and pushes me against the door. His hands slide over my head to lock the room just as his lips descend on mine. I surrender to his passion with a loud moan, feeling my entire body spark to life when our lips meet in a scorching kiss. He devours my mouth hungrily, his hardness pressing between my legs. He's aroused already.

Ronan slides his tongue between my lips, French kissing me in my bedroom, his fingers sliding under my dress. I'm wearing a short pink dress, and I skipped the underwear so that we could save time. His fingers rub against my needy pussy, feeling wetness coat them. He grunts into my mouth, pressing my ass to the door as he deepens the kiss. His fingers slide between my swollen pussy lips, teasing my clit with one finger while he pushes his middle finger inside my wet and willing cunt.

"Oh…" My brain short-circuits at the contact, my fleshy walls gripping him. I've been dying to feel his cock between my legs since that first time. He fucked me all night and left me sore for a week, but once I recovered, I knew I wanted it again. Sex has unleashed a beast in me, a beast only he can tame. He kisses me hard, pushing another finger into my channel to warm me up. His thumb plays with my clit, rubbing my hard little button to stimulate my pleasure. My nipples tighten, sensitive against the fabric of my dress. My pussy squeezes my tutor's fingers and he breaks the kiss with a growl.

"I missed you, baby." He is breathless. "I've been thinking about you all week. God, that wet pussy has me in a chokehold." His fingers stroke my inner walls, and my hips push forward, riding him. He smiles. "Is my baby girl greedy for her Daddy's cock already? Look how you're riding my fingers."

"I've been dreaming of this all week," I confess. "I've been dying to feel you come inside me."

"God, you're addicted be being bred," he rasps, pulling his fingers out of my cunt that are wet with my juices.

"Make me your little cum slut, Daddy."

"That's exactly what I plan to do." His eyes twinkle as he reaches for the back zipper of my dress and pulls it down. "Strip for me, baby."

I take off the dress, desperate to feel his skin against mine. Ronan lets out a pleased grunt when he sees me buck-naked. "No bra, no panties. You're becoming a bad girl." His knuckle reaches forward to stroke my hard tips. His cum-slicked fingers touch my aroused nipple and my core burns when he spreads my juices all over my nipples, circling my puffy areolae with his thick fingers. "I love it when you're all hard for me, baby. It makes sucking on those titties more fun." He deposits the remaining cum on my other nipple before wiping his wet fingers over my breasts. Then, he puts his hand under my knee and hoists me up. My eyes widen at that, enjoying it when he carries me to my bed bridal-style.

He lays me down on my bed and begins removing his clothes. Within seconds, he's as naked as me, his thick cock aroused and hard for me. I spread my legs, flashing my pussy at my tutor who grunts, using his hand to stroke his throbbing, velvety dick that's curving upward at the sight of my fleshy, pink walls. "I missed this pussy so much," he grunts. "So pretty like a rose."

Ronan climbs over me on the bed, making the mattress slump with his weight. His thick dick hands down, his balls full of cum. I lick my lips, wanting him to fill me with a cream pie. My tutor brings the swollen tip of his cock to my slit and teases it.

"Who owns this pussy, little dove?" His voice is possessive.

"You do." I close my eyes, enjoying how it feels to have his pre-cum coat my intimate folds. His masculine scent is so seductive, pulling me deeper into his orbit.

Ronan pushes his cock inside me and I bite down on my lower lip to keep from screaming. His hard member slides between my slippery folds, filling me up inch by inch. The stretch is delicious, the sensation of his cock plugging up my pussy so addictive. It's way more pleasurable than the first time, and I don't want him to stop.

"You're still so tight, Elsie. I want to be in your pussy all the time." He skewers me with his dick until he's balls-deep inside my cunt. I open my eyes, filled with Ronan's dick, watching him observe my naked body. He lowers his head, closing his mouth around one nipple and suckling. My cunt clenches around him, making him groan and bite my tip. He licks my pussy juices from my teat, making more pleasure vibrate between my legs.

"Ronan…please…"

"Please what, baby?" He licks my hard nub with his tongue before moving to the other and suckling on it. My mind scrambles with him inside me and his mouth on my sensitive tips.

"Please, fuck me." Flashes of light fill my vision.

Ronan begins moving inside me just as he sucks my other nipple. His cock is eager and hard, swollen to its full size in my channel. It squelches in and out of my hole in hard, deep thrusts, making my tits bounce. I arch my back, feeding him my nipple and squishing his face with my breasts. He grabs my tit and massages it, making an orgasm building in my core. Ronan pulls his mouth away, grabbing my hips, and then, he rails me hard.

His cock grinds deep into my pussy, scraping my inner walls. He repeatedly assaults my G-spot, the friction between our bodies driving me out of my mind. He uses my body like a toy, fucking and pleasuring me. His balls spank my ass, his need for me wild and uncontrolled as he pounds me hard.

"Ronan…" I come on his cock, my walls massaging his dick as he continues to grind into me. My body explodes into ribbons of pleasure. Bliss balloons through my core, filling every single cell with light. It feels so good to come for him.

"Baby, I'm coming." Ronan grunts before he climaxes. Ropes of hot cum fill my belly, taking the experience to another level. "Take it all in like a good cum slut," he roars. "Every single drop."

His words make me hot. I hold onto him as we climax together, him filling me up to the brim with a cream pie. He's full of cum thanks to two weeks of not touching me. I can feel it gushing inside me like water out of a hose. I suck it all up like a good girl, wanting to nurture his seed deep in my womb and have his babies.

Ronan collapses breathless on the bed a few minutes later. It's only been twenty minutes since he arrived and he's already come inside me. My tutor pulls his cock out of my pussy and I watch a bead of cum slide out of my pussy. Ronan gathers it up with his thumb and pushes it back into my pussy, making me groan.

"God, breeding you is the best feeling in the world. I thought I'd go crazy if I didn't touch you again." He touches my swollen pussy, feeling the aftershocks of my orgasm.

"I missed you too. I've been looking out of my window all day for you." Ronan pulls me close to him, and I melt into his embrace.

His fingers rub over my lower lip that's bleeding. He kisses me, licking my blood from my lips. I put my legs around him, threading my limbs with his powerful thighs as our lips remain locked in a kiss. Every time he's near me, I feel so much better. Can you crave a person's existence?

Ronan licks my lower lip, sucking it like a fleshy fruit as he makes my bleeding stop. Removing his lips, he kisses my jaw, all the way down to my neck where he's left a little mark. I've been having a hard time hiding it all week, but Ronan makes me feel all better when he kisses me there.

"What would your parents think if they knew I'd been

fucking you during our tutoring sessions instead of teaching you math?" His voice vibrates in the crook of my neck.

"Who cares what they think? I liked being fucked by you a lot more than I like Math."

"You're a bad student," he says, finding my ass and pinching it. I cry out and he sucks on my sensitive spot again, making me feel so good. "But you're the perfect girlfriend."

Girlfriend? Really? Did I hear that word right?

"You want me to be your girlfriend?" I ask boldly, running my hands all over his defined arms. I swear he looks fitter every time I see him.

"No," he admits, and my heart sinks for a moment. "I'd rather have you as my wife." My eyes widen and Ronan stops kissing me. He gazes into my eyes, touching my cheek with his thumb. "I've been thinking, Elsie."

"Oh?" I can't even hear his voice above the beating of my heart.

"I don't think this is a fling. I'm way too into you for it to be a passing fancy."

"Ronan…."

"I know I'm not good enough for you, but I only want you, baby girl. There are a million reasons why we shouldn't be together, and there's only one why we should."

"What's what?" I ask.

"I love you," he says.

My heart just freezes. "Ronan…do you…mean that?"

"I heard you that night," he says. "I wasn't sure of my feelings back then, but I am now. You're the one I want, Elsie. I want to build a home with you, baby. I want to give you a safe space where you can bloom." Tears fill my eyes. "I want you in my bed every night, and I want to be by your side when you're sad." He puts his big palm on my stomach. "I want to fill this beautiful belly with our babies and make love to you while you grow them inside your stomach. No matter how you look, I'll always love you."

The floodgates of my heart open, and I begin crying in earnest now. "Are you…proposing to me right now?"

I can't believe Ronan is proposing to me while we're naked in bed, his cum inside me. But then again, I can't think of a better moment.

"I am," he admits. I guess I should do this the right way." He leans over, grabbing his discarded pants from the floor. Digging into the pocket, he pulls out a velvet ring box. Ronan rolls off the bed, holding out his hand to me. I take it and stand, my legs shaky and my eyes blurry. He goes down on one knee, naked as the day we were born, and holds up a gleaming golden band. "Will you marry me, Elsie?"

I just stop breathing for a second. Tears stream down my eyes and I know deep in my heart that this is everything I've ever wanted.

"I wanted to talk to your father before I asked you, but as you know, he might not accept us. I wanted to be sure about your feelings first. I know you're young, and there are still many things you want to do, and I promise you that I'll always support you, no matter what you want to do." He pauses, smiling at me. "I love you, Elsie. No matter how hard I tried to fight it, I couldn't. I need you in my life, baby. Please, say yes."

I gaze down at the velvet box and choke. "Ronan…I can't believe….oh my gosh…" I hurriedly wipe my tears away, not wanting to ruin the moment. "You're everything I've dreamed of. I only want to be your wife, your lover, and have your children. Yes, I will marry you. You've made me so happy, Ronan. There's no one else I'd rather spend my life with."

"Thank you, baby." Ronan smiles plucking the golden band from the box. I give him my shaking fingers and he slips the ring onto my hand. Then, he stands up and kisses me. I sink into my future husband's embrace, knowing this is everything I've ever wanted.

"We can get married as soon as you graduate school and you could move in with me," he says when we stop kissing. "I'll start to look for some off-campus housing. It'll be temporary, just until I get my degree, and then, we can find a permanent home. I promise to get you a diamond ring once I get a job."

"I don't want a diamond ring, I only want you," I say, resting my head on his chest. "I never want to be apart from you."

He holds my hip, his palms rubbing my belly. "And in case you get pregnant," I look up. "Which you definitely will considering how much I like breeding you." I smile. "I've got some money saved up to take care of our baby. It should be enough until I get a job."

He's thought about everything. I don't care Ronan isn't rich. He's smart and hard-working and most importantly, he loves me. I know he'll find a way to make it work.

"I trust you," I tell him. "And I don't need a lot of money. I want to spend the rest of my life creating a happy, loving family with you."

"Me too, baby. I want to spend my life loving my beautiful baby girl." He kisses my temple and I linger in his naked kisses for long moments before it's time for our tutoring session to end.

His ring on my finger, Ronan gets dressed. Before leaving, he says, "Let's keep the engagement a secret for now. I'll talk to your father once your exams are over."

I nod. I don't even need Dad's approval. In my heart, I already belong to Ronan.

He kisses me goodbye, and leaves and I watch him disappear into his car from my bedroom window. As he drives away, I imagine being in that car next to him as his wife.

My heart feels so full and happy.

CHAPTER 7
RONAN

I apply for my hundredth job in one week, eager to find something. After I proposed to Elsie, I knew that I wanted to give my baby girl the best life possible, and for that, I needed a job that paid well while giving me enough time to spend with my future wife. I watch her sitting quietly in her room through the cameras, mesmerized by her lovely face as she knits her blonde eyebrows together, focusing on a math problem. Her blue eyes gaze around, not knowing that I'm watching her.

Her math exam is three days away and I've been tutoring her almost every day. However, we don't get to do anything naughty since her parents are always in the house. We're keeping the engagement a secret until I get a job but when I come to her room, Elsie always wears her ring and I hold her hand while we study together. Of course, most of our time is spent kissing and making out, but she's been studying hard so that she can make me proud. Elsie will graduate in a few weeks and I can't wait to make her my wife and be with her after that.

Going through my e-mails, I notice that a new one has

popped up. Eagerly, I click it to find that one of the companies I applied for has invited me for an interview. Joy rushes through me, knowing that I'm one step closer to making Elsie my wife. I immediately fill the details out and schedule the interview for next week. Just as I slump back on the chair, I notice that Elsie disappears from the screen.

I take a sip of water and fill in more job applications. Before I know it, it's time for lunch. I stand up and stretch, looking forward to grabbing lunch when I hear voices outside my door. The doorbell rings and I walk out of my room to get to the main door. When I open it, my eyes widen.

"Hi." Elsie stands in front of me, wearing a blue crop top and shorts. Her hair is tied back in a ponytail. She smells of sugar and candy and looks good enough to eat. I grab her waist and pull her in, kissing her lips before she can say anything more. Our bodies mold together naturally, her soft tits pressing against my hard chest as she wraps her legs around my waist and gives in to my kiss. I taste her soft, sweet lips, sucking on them like I need them to live. I see her every day, and it's like this every time. I can't live without her anymore. It was stupid to think I could ever breed her and let her go. She's my greatest obsession.

When I release her lips, coming up for air, she gazes into my eyes, her baby blues darkening with lust. "I got bored studying. I thought I'd spend some time with my fiancé instead." She raises her finger, showing me her ring. My cock hardens with possessiveness, loving the sight of my future wife wearing my ring.

"Mmmm…you're always welcome here, baby." I kiss her lips, carrying her to my room with her legs still around my waist. I push her down on the bed and climb over her, my cock hardening at the sight of my beautiful fiancee. He clings to me, letting me push my hands under her top and knead her breasts through her bra. "God, you're like a drug. I'm always dying for another hit of you." I push her top up and suckle her nipples through the fabric of her bra. She moans in my arms, her hips grinding on my erection eagerly. Just as I grab at her waistband, my stomach emits a loud groan.

Elsie stops, her lips curving into a smile. I continue suckling her nipples, but she tugs at my shoulder. "You're hungry."

"I'm hungry for you," I push her bra cups down and take one bare nipple between my mouth. She whimpers as I suckle her tip, squeezing her ass through her shorts. But when my stomach growls again, the moment is broken. "Damn."

She smiles at me. "Go get lunch," she says. "I can wait. I don't want my future husband starving to death."

Elsie is so sweet. I want her so bad right now, but I know I've been starving since morning and need to eat. "I'm sorry," I say, kissing her lips lightly. "I've been busy applying for jobs all morning. I'll go get some food. Do you want anything?"

"Some ice cream," she says. "I need something sweet to revive me."

I kiss her collarbone before climbing off her. "Wait here. I'll be back in a few minutes."

She nods, watching me grab a hoodie and put it on. She lies there on my bed, pulling her bra up over her glistening nipples that carry my scent. She adjusts her top as I leave the room, watching her every step of the way.

I make a quick run down the street, grabbing some Mexican along with the ice cream Elsie requested. Hurriedly jogging back to my girl, I realize it's been over fifteen minutes. There was a line at the ice cream place, but I couldn't disappoint Elsie, could I? I unlock the front door with my key, carrying bags of food, a big smile on my face. Once I eat my lunch, I'm going to fuck Elsie all afternoon until she's rejuvenated and sore.

But as soon as I open my bedroom door, I sense a shift in the air.

Elsie sits on my chair, scrolling my laptop, which I left open. Instantly, fear hits me.

"Elsie...." She turns and there's hurt in her eyes. My eyes move to the image on the screen and my blood freezes. It's a live video of Elsie's room. One of the maids is cleaning it and she can see everything in clear detail. Next to the small window is a video player with a sex tape of me eating Elsie's pussy, the one I filmed the first time I made her come. She watches the sex tape roll on, every moan and whisper clear.

"What is this, Ronan?" There's distrust in her eyes, and I hate it. "Why do you have a video of us…making you…and why can you see everything that's going on in my house?"

My fist clenches, realizing it's time I told her the truth. I place the food bags on my bed and take a step toward her, but she suddenly stands up, backing off an inch. My heart drops at how scared she's of me.

"Elsie, baby, listen to me. It's not what you think."

"You've been stalking me." She licks her lips. "For how long? Are there other videos of us having sex?" Panic echoes through her skull, and I know she's thinking of the worst-case scenarios. I rake a hand through my hair. "Answer me, Ronan."

"Yes. There are other videos of us. Of you touching yourself in your room." I exhale sharply.

"How? I didn't even know I was being filmed." There's betrayal in her eyes and I know I fucked up.

"I put up cameras in your room," I confess. "I just wanted to make sure you were safe."

Elsie is shocked, but her hand clicks something else that pops up on the screen. She doesn't read it, though, focused on me instead. "That's why…that's how you know I had those scars. That night when Bill tried to touch me…you came so fast…did you know because you saw it here?"

I nod. "I was furious he tried to touch my girl. I couldn't stop myself from coming to you."

Elsie covers her face with her hands. "Oh my god, how long has this been going on for?" Her blue gaze is cold as ice when it turns to me. "Are there cameras in other parts of the house?"

I don't want to lie to her. "Two years. Ever since I started tutoring you."

Her eyes go wide. "So, every time I..." She drags in a deep breath. "I touched myself, you knew?"

I nod. "I loved watching you call out my name when you made yourself come." My voice is low and sexy, but she doesn't respond to it. "Every morning, I watched you dress, and undress, and it made me feel like I was there with you. I wanted to be part of your life."

"But...you always pushed me away. You said I was just a student."

"You were underage, baby girl. I didn't want to do anything you weren't ready for."

"So, what? You watched me instead?" She shudders. Her fingers slide over the mouse and she clicks another window and realizes I've bugged other rooms too. Her eyes move to the screen and she realizes I'm watching the hallway, George's room, and her parents too. "Oh my god, you've bugged my whole house." Her hands shake on the mouse. "What's this?" She leans forward, reading the records of George that I have.

"Baby, that's—" I stop short when she finds a video of George on the screen. I freeze when it begins to play, showing George kicking a boy. I've been gathering evidence of his bullying over the years. I've bugged him too and his regular visits to the Mulligan house have helped me get more information on him.

"This is...my brother..." She turns to me. "Why do you have videos of him?"

I grab the edge of the table hard as Elsie clicks another

stumbled on your videos today, would you have continued lying to me?"

"I wanted to tell you," I admit. "But after I asked you to be my wife, I forgot about it."

"Forgot? You've been watching me every day, Ronan. Even moments before I came here....you were stalking me."

Stalking. That's an ugly word.

"I don't want to lose you, Elsie. That's why I didn't tell you. Of course, I would tell you once we got married—"

"Once we got married?" she scoffs. "You're just like my parents. Did you think I wouldn't have any option once I was trapped in marriage with you?" She cries, brushing away her tears. "God, I was such a fool. I thought you really loved me."

"I do love you," I tell her. "And I'd kill myself before I ever made you unhappy."

Elsie shakes her head. "I don't trust you anymore, Ronan." She reaches for the wedding band on her finger and pulls it off. My heart turns to stone when she places it on the desk. "I can't marry you, not like this."

"Elsie, baby...listen to me...." My body is frozen in place as she moves toward the door. I grab her before I can think, enveloping her in a back hug. My hands squeeze her body, hoping she realizes how much I want her.

"Baby, don't go." I hold her tight. "I love you." My lips kiss the back of her neck and she shivers under me, responding to my kiss. "Tell me what I can do to make it okay."

For a moment, she melts into my embrace, and I think she's going to give me a chance, but then, her hands come to rest on my arms, and she says, "You're hurting me."

I let her go reluctantly and she turns around to meet my eye, one hand on the doorknob. "Don't ever contact me again."

And then, she opens the door and leaves. I'm left stunned, standing in place as I hear the main door lock.

Elsie is gone and it's all my fault.

I sink to the ground, regretting the day I came up with this sick revenge plan. Back then, I could've never imagined that I'd find the love of my life in Elsie, the very woman I planned to destroy. Blackness covers my vision as I sink to the floor and let the first tear escape my eye.

CHAPTER 8
ELSIE
THREE WEEKS LATER—

I look at the bookshelf in front of me, my face between my legs. My exams are done and I'm all set to graduate, but I feel like shit. I gaze down at my phone which is flooded with messages from Ronan. He messages me several times a day to make sure I'm doing okay. A big bouquet of roses sits on my table, making me feel even worse. Ronan got it delivered this morning, and I had to lie to my Mom and Dad about it being from Bill.

After I left Ronan, George said he'd convinced Bill to give me another chance. My parents think I've been talking to him over the phone, but they're wrong. Bill just sent me one text saying he'd like to take me on a date and I haven't even replied to him yet. Ronan, on the other hand, has been blowing up the phone.

Ronan: Good morning. How's my baby girl doing today? I saw these roses and thought of you.

He says that he loves me several times a day, trying to break down the walls between us. The messages bleed into one another, reminding me of the time when I used to persistently text him. There are no dick pics, however, only confessions of love.

Ronan: I'm sorry. I'm going to keep saying sorry until you believe it.

Ronan: How was your math exam? I know my baby girl aced it.

Even though I haven't seen him in weeks, he's all I think about. I sit in bed, my heart in pieces. He calls me at least twenty times a day, but I never answer. I gaze ahead, seeing nothing but a harmless book where Ronan's camera was. I wish he could watch me right now, falling apart and crying all the time.

It's been three weeks since we broke up since I returned his ring and left him, and I still feel the heartbreak like it was yesterday.

My exams are done and I should be excited because my parents are planning my wedding with Bill. Except, my heart hurts. My stomach hurts. My body hurts. Everything hurts. Another message lights up my phone and my eyes eagerly devour it.

Ronan: I love you, baby girl.

My heart squeezes with pain. I want to go to him. I want him to hold me as I fall apart, but I can't.

After I came back home from Ronan's dorm, I cried for hours. When the tears dried, I realized I wasn't crying because he'd lied to me, I was crying because I'd been stupid. What George did to Ronan's brother is unforgivable and I don't know if I can be with him, knowing how my family messed up his brother. He's determined, strong, and single-minded, and the fact that he found it in his heart to love me, the sister of the boy who drove his brother to death, is something I can't even comprehend.

A wave of nausea fills my stomach when I see a picture of Ronan on my phone, his sexy smile and those bright silver eyes filling my gaze. Longing fills my heart. Now that I've had some time to think, I understand why he did what he did. I'd do the same if I'd lost my brother. Hell, I'd probably

MY TUTOR, MY STALKER 79

set my house on fire instead of patiently stalking me. Now, I know what it feels like to lose someone you love.

I've wanted to apologize to him since that day. I know he stalked me, but when I saw those videos on his computer, I felt my pussy clench. The thought of Ronan being so obsessed with me, of stalking me weirdly turns me on. Even now, I want him to see me as I take off my clothes, as I wish for his big hands to caress my wet pussy. His burning desire is the reason I'm attracted to him. He's the kind of man who'd go to the ends of the earth for the woman he loves, and that is what makes him so sexy. Deep inside, I know he is different. He's broken and obsessive, and I love that part of him too. I love that he's obsessed with me.

A knock resounds on my door and I hurriedly wipe away my tears, reaching for the knob. But when I open it, I see George standing on the other side.

"George?"

"Hey, Bill says you haven't been responding to his texts. Mom and Dad are literally planning your wedding. Can you at least try, after all that I went through to get you a date with him?" I hate that his tone is accusing. Now that I look at him carefully, I realize he's always been selfish. "The boys are going out tonight. You can join us if you want. Bill's girlfriend will be there too."

"Bill has a girlfriend?" My eyes widen.

"Yeah, since the start of college. She's really hot too."

"But…he's supposed to be marrying me."

"Elsie." George raises his hand, patting my hair. "You know how high society marriages work. Fidelity isn't part of the agreement. Bill will marry you, get you pregnant and once you have two kids, you can get your pleasure elsewhere. A man can't give up his needs just because he has a wife."

I scoff. I can't believe what I'm hearing. "That's called cheating, brother."

"Well, cheating is a part of marriage," he says. "Now, if

you want Bill to take you seriously, you need to show up tonight."

My heart thuds violently. What was I thinking? There's no way I can go through with a marriage like that. Not when there's a man who loves me more than anything, a man who gave up on revenge to choose me. My eyes get a little glassy.

"Why're you crying?" George asks. "You've been a little mushy these days. Is it because you're graduating?"

"It's PMS." I lie.

"Well, I hope to see you at the party tonight. I'll send you the location." George bows out before I display any more feminine emotions. Alone inside my room, everything becomes very clear.

I never belonged in this house. I still don't. There is no way I can choose a future with Bill. Not when I still love Ronan.

I lock the door and open my drawer to find the camera I hid away. I didn't want Mom and Dad to know what Ronan had done, so I just debugged my room and hid all the cameras. However, as I pull one out, and place it on the bookshelf, a thrill travels through my spine. This time, my stalker will know that I'm watching him too.

I close the window blinds and pull off my clothes until I'm standing in nothing but my bra and panties. I chose a black one that contrasts my pale skin, drawing attention to my pink nipples. I set the camera up and then, I turn it on. A red light flashes, letting me know it's recording. I sit back on my bed, turning my ass to the camera as I reach for my phone. I push my bra cups down, my nipples popping out. Turning to the camera, I touch myself, rolling and playing with my nipples until they're aroused into hard little beads. As I thrust my chest up, watching my tits jiggle, I know Ronan is watching me. When a message pings, I smile.

Ronan: What the fuck are you doing, Elsie?

I pluck my nipples again, smiling at the camera before I

MY TUTOR, MY STALKER   81

unclasp my bra and throw it to the floor. My perky breasts bounce free, my nipples hard for Ronan's gaze.

Ronan: Fuck, baby, I've missed seeing those perfect tits.

Oh yeah, he's into it. I move my chest, watching my breasts jiggle. I can imagine him getting hard, I can hear his sexy growl. He always sounds like that when he's dying to possess me. I cup my tits, squeezing them for him.

Ronan: Please tell me this is what I think it is.

His words are hopeful, desperate and I want to tell him that he's right. But I want to tease him first.

Elsie: I'm putting on a show for my stalker. I just realized I love being watched.

I wait for his reply, hopefully, touching myself. My pussy begins to get moist, the need for my stalker filling me up. Just the image of him makes me go hot all over.

Ronan: Yeah? I could watch you all day.

It's when I read those words that I realize how much he loves me. He must've spent a lot of time watching me doing boring things like homework and just sleeping.

I reach for my panties and pull them off too. When I open my legs, baring my wet pussy, a smile lights up my face. I reach for my phone, turning my body around so that my ass is in the air, my pussy in direct line with the camera. My bare tits hit the bedsheets, my phone in hand as I type out my message.

Elsie: Are you touching yourself to the sight of me?

Ronan: No, I'm driving to your house so that I can touch you for real.

My pussy clenches on camera at the thought of seeing him again. God, I've missed him so much.

Ronan: Be naked when I arrive.

His possessive commands are making slick drip down my slit. I push my fingers between my legs, touching my swollen folds and giving him a sex tape he'll remember. My pussy feels extra-sensitive when I rub my clit, making me wonder if the reason I'm feeling so needy is because I haven't been touched by Ronan in weeks. But then, another idea comes to me.

I instantly shut my legs, rolling down on the mattress with panic filling me. I roll off the bed, reaching for my calendar and counting the days from my last period. It's been over a month.

Inhaling a deep breath, I sit down on my chair, my pussy buzzing. I open my drawer and raise the bottom compartment to find two pregnancy tests after the first time Ronan made love to me. I was so into him breeding me that I dreamed about the day these came out positive and I could show it to him. I reach for the camera and turn it off, not wanting to kill the surprise. Then, I carry my pregnancy tests and head into my bathroom.

Ten minutes later, I'm done taking both of them.

The result is unanimous.

You're pregnant.

The words stare at me, changing my life beyond belief. Joy bubbles in my heart, tears running down my eyes as I clutch my pregnancy tests close to my heart. At this moment, I feel nothing but gratitude. Everything I've wished for is here. I grab my robe, putting the tests into the pocket of the robe.

The doorbell rings just as I finish tying my sash.

Ronan is here.

I step out of the bathroom and wait for him to come to my door. When I hear a sharp knock, I slowly reach for the handle and open it.

"Elsie…" Ronan stands at the door, breathless, his silver eyes fixed on me. Behind him, I can hear Mom saying he left something in my room. Ronan gets in and shuts the door, but doesn't lock it. He also doesn't hug me and kiss me the way he usually does. "Was that…baby, are you really giving me another chance?"

I nod. "I was waiting for you." I take a step toward him

and he closes the distance between us. His fingers are an inch from me, but he doesn't touch me.

"I'm sorry," his words are thick with remorse. "I'm so sorry for ever hurting you, for disappointing you, and breaking your heart. I know you can't trust me right now, but I meant it when I said I'd do anything to make it up to you. I love you, Elsie. That hasn't changed, and that's never going to change no matter how far you push me away. You're the one for me, baby girl. I'll wait for you forever."

His words are ragged with emotion, making my pussy spark with need.

"Anything?" I loop my hands around his neck, molding my body to his as I get up on my tiptoes. Our lips are so close to touching, and I want to taste him so bad. "You'd do anything to win my trust again?"

"Anything," he affirms with labored breaths, watching me as I run my finger over his jaw. "Just tell me what you need me to do."

"I want you to marry me," I tell him. "Spend the rest of your life making it up to me. Love me every day, Ronan, just like I love you."

With that sexy growl, he seals my lips with his. His hands come around me, holding me close and devouring my mouth as my feet are lifted off the ground by his powerful hands. He cups my ass and holds me close, tasting my tongue with his, making me feel so complete and happy. If I didn't know it before, I know it now. I love this man with everything I've got in me.

Ronan's lips part a few seconds later, nibbling on my lower lip. His eyelashes open, watching me with lust.

"Are you sure this is a punishment?" he asks. "Because to me, it feels a lot like a dream come true. Loving you is the easiest thing in the world."

When he looks at me like that, I feel like the only woman in the world. How did I ever think I could give this up?

Ronan has changed my life. He's given me something I thought I'd never have—true love. I never even dared to hope I'd be desired by a man like this.

"Give me your ring and ask me again," I tell him. "Please."

Ronan swallows, reluctantly letting go of my body. He reaches into his jeans pocket and pulls out the golden wedding band he proposed to me with. "I've been carrying it around with me, hoping I'd get a chance to do this again." He goes down on one knee, his eyes sincere when he looks at me. "Elsie Mulligan, will you marry me and make me the happiest man alive?"

"Yes," I whisper. "I think I will."

Ronan rises to his feet, slipping the wedding band on my finger. And then, he picks me up and throws me on the bed, kissing my mouth until all I know is his scent.

"I never thought you'd give me another chance," he says when we stop kissing. "Every day without you was a nightmare. I promised myself that I'd never keep anything from you if you chose me again." His lips nibble on my lower lip and I moan in his arms.

"I regretted breaking up with you just one day later. I got through my exams like a zombie, and then, I knew I'd made a mistake. The thing is, I felt bad for what my family did to your brother. Once I got over the initial shock, I understood why you wanted revenge. What George did to your brother was wrong and he deserves to be punished for it."

He kisses my lips tenderly. "It doesn't matter anymore. I don't care about what George did. All I want is you. You're the only thing that matters, Elsie. I was made to love you, baby, and that's what I plan to do for the rest of our lives." He kisses my cheek, my jaw, and my nose, letting me know how much he wants me.

I touch his dark hair, cupping his jaw until our eyes meet.

MY TUTOR, MY STALKER   85

With a naughty smile, I add, "You know, I'm really into stalking now."

"Yeah?" he asks, leaning forward to take a sip of my lips.

"Ummm…The thought of my hot husband watching me secretly turns me on. Maybe we should install cameras in our bedroom once we get married. I have a lot of ideas to keep my man entertained."

"Damn, I'd be too distracted with sexy videos of my wife to work." He breathes, taking my palms in his and kissing them. "Are you sure you wouldn't mind the invasion of privacy?"

"Not if I knew you were looking at me." I smile.

His hand slips under my robe, cupping my bare ass. "Thank you for giving me a chance, baby. I promise I'll make you happy."

"You already make me so happy," I say. "I can't wait to live the rest of my life without you."

"Me neither." His fingers slip between my legs, teasing my wet pussy. When I moan, he asks, "I thought I told you to stay naked. You're too overdressed."

"There was an emergency," I reply, putting my hand over his when he tries to tug at my sash. "There's something I need to tell you."

When he raises his eyebrows, I dig into my pocket and pull out the pregnancy tests. "I've got a little surprise for you, husband." His eyes widen when he sees what I'm holding out.

"Is that—" He takes it from me, turning it over to read the results. "Is this for real?" His throat is thick with emotion, his eyes glassy. "Oh my god…Are you…are we…" He shakes his head.

"We're going to be parents," I tell him, taking his hand and placing it over my belly. "You bred me well, Daddy."

He looks on the verge of tears, his big palm traveling over my stomach. "I can't believe this. This has got to be the happiest day of my life." He dips his head and kisses my stomach, and I run my fingers through his hair, holding him close. "Baby girl, you're the best thing that's ever happened to me." He buries his face in my stomach and I know he's elated. "I'm going to be a dad…we're having a kid together… it feels like a dream."

"The best kind of dream," I tell him. "Because you're in it with me."

He smiles, getting off the bed and then, he lifts me up, carrying me in his arms.

"What are you doing?" I ask.

"Let's go tell your parents," he says. "Your dad needs to know that I'm marrying his daughter right now and taking her home."

"What? I thought you said we'd wait until graduation."

"It's too far away. I want the mother of my child next to me all the time."

"Aren't you possessive?" I tease.

"That's why you love me," he fires back, kissing my lips as he kicks the door open. I hear a maid shriek as she watches Ronan carry me down the stairs.

"What if Dad says no?" I ask him, looping my arms around his neck.

"Then, I'll carry you out of this house just like this. There's no way I'm ever letting you go again."

I smile. "I think I'd like that."

CHAPTER 9
RONAN
THREE YEARS LATER—

My pregnant wife sits in our son's room with me, reading him a bedtime story. Her body pressed against mine, my hand on her shoulder, I watch our two-and-a-half-year-old son, Kayden's eyes droop. He has his mother's blue eyes and my dark hair and he's so adorable, trying to sleep in his tiny bed.

"And then the frog said to the princess," Elsie pauses, her eyes shutting as she winces. I gaze down at where she's clutching her breast, gently massaging it as she smiles at our son. Her long, satin nightgown molds to her sexy Mommy body, showing off her new curves. Elsie is lactating and she's been feeding Kayden ever since he was born. However, he's started to wean off and she's still making a lot of milk. I gaze at her engorged tits that are massive, resting heavily against her six-month-old baby bump.

"Let me," I take the book from her, gently rubbing her stomach as she smiles up at me. I read out the rest of the story to our son as my wife holds his hand, caressing his hair as he drifts off to sleep. When he begins to snore, I shut the book and turn to Elsie. She's so beautiful, her body lush and fertile like a goddess. Even without makeup, her face looks ethereal, wispy blonde hair framing her feminine features. We've been married for three years, but every time I look at her, I want to kiss her. Elsie leans forward, pressing a kiss on our son's head.

"He's asleep." She turns to me and I stand up, putting the book back on the shelf before extending my hand to her and helping my wife stand up. She takes it, standing next to me. Silently, we watch our son snoring in his bed. My palm rests on her swollen belly, rubbing it gently. Kayden is going to have a sister soon.

"He's adorable when he's sleeping." My son has a lot of energy and I spend my evenings and weekends playing with him. It's quite a workout. I dip my head down, still keeping my hands around my wife's stomach, and drop a kiss on my son's head. "Good night, Kayden."

I thread my fingers in my wife's and we both quietly tiptoe out of our son's room, the camera turned on to keep an eye on his movements. Once I close the door, I grab my wife's waist and pull her close. Her baby bump collides against my stomach, the movement making her engorged breasts jiggle a little.

"Ronan...." Her beautiful face is all mine. My wedding band glints on her finger and she cups my face with her soft hands. I turn my face to kiss it. She wears my ring every day, reminding me of the vows I made to the woman I love the most in the world.

"I've missed you, baby." I was at work all day and I only get to be with her at night. It's been three years since we got married. After I asked her father for her hand and he refused, I carried her out of her house and we never looked back. Elsie and I got married the next day and she moved in with me in my dorm until I found a house. Soon after I graduated, I started working a prestigious job in the city and made enough money to support my wife and our growing family.

"I've missed you all day, Mrs, Jackson." I touch her belly

and lean forward, pressing a kiss on her juicy, welcoming lips. She moans, gently putting her hands around me as I take her lips in a sweet kiss. Elsie loves it when I call her by my last name, letting the whole world know that she's mine. We're always needy for each other. That hasn't changed. I kiss my wife tenderly, feeling love light up my heart.

"Me too." Elsie's lips are wet when our mouths part. "I've been waiting for you to come back home all day. There's something I wanted to you to see."

She takes my hand and drags me to our bedroom. We bought our own house this year after I got a huge performance bonus. With our own home and a growing family, life is perfect. Our three-bedroom family home is our little sanctuary, a place my love and I have built together. I walk through the hallway, reaching for the handle of our bedroom. When we step in, a huge bed greets me. We've got our matching nightstands and closets on either side of the room along with an en-suite bathroom where we've had shower sex a few times. Our house is filled with happy memories of our love.

Making me sit on the bed, Elsie walks over to her nightstand and pulls out her iPad. "I saw this while I was reading the news this morning." She pushes the iPad in my direction and I read the headline.

Mulligan Enterprises Under Investigation

There's a picture of George in handcuffs and the article details how he was found guilty of fraud, putting the whole company under the radar of the IRS. I blink up at her, wondering if she's showing me this because she's worried about her family. After Elsie left with me, none of the Mulligans contacted us. If she missed her family, she didn't show it. But I wonder if I took away something precious from her.

"Your revenge," she says. "It happened."

"What?" I blink. After Elsie and I got married, I gave up on avenging my brother. Loving her took up my days and nights, and I no longer had any time to think about her past.

With a baby on the way, my focus was on creating a blissful future with my wife. Mom came for my graduation and met Elsie. She also takes care of Kayden sometimes and Elsie loves her.

"George is going to jail. I know it's not for bullying, but it's justice, right?" Her blue eyes meet me, wide and knowing.

"Elsie, he's your brother. Are you okay with him going to jail?"

"I'm Mrs. Jackson now," she replies. "I've got nothing to do with that family. All I care about is you." She places her hand in the crook of my arm, laying her head to rest on my shoulder. "When you married me and gave up on revenge, I felt bad because I'd taken away the chance to avenge your brother's death. I know what George did was wrong, but because he's family, I couldn't stand by your side. But when I read the article this morning, I couldn't help but feel that it was karma working. Nobody should have to go through what your brother went through."

I gaze into her eyes, in awe of Elsie's empathetic nature. "Baby, do you know how rare you are? Not many people would be okay with seeing their family ruined, even if it was for a just cause."

"You're my only family now, Ronan," she says. "You're the one who makes me happy. My mom, dad, and brother only saw me as a pawn, not a person. Living with you has made me realize how much better life can be. I'm glad you took me away from that house." She rubs her stomach, smiling. "I'm glad to be yours, Daddy. I used to live in fear every day in that house, waiting for my tutor to visit on the weekends so that I could feel better."

"You'll always have me, baby. You know that." I kiss her lips, put the iPad away, and lay her down on the bed. "Now let me kiss that baby bump. I've been dying to touch my wife all day."

"I'm all yours, husband," she says as I pull up the hem of her nightgown, stripping her bare. In a flash, Elsie is naked, her large, swollen belly bared to my gaze. I remove my shirt and pants and throw them on the floor before climbing over my wife's body. Elsie's gaze travels to my throbbing dick that's semi-hard just from the sight of her. I press my man meat against her swollen belly, reminding her who bred her and knocked her up. Her small fingers reach up, gently stroking my cock and making an ache pulse deep in my core. Her hands slide up and down my veiny shaft, rubbing my pre-cum around my tip when I begin to leak. "I love taking my husband's cock." A drop of pre-cum falls on her big belly and she hisses. "You've seeded me good, Daddy."

I groan. "Fuck, baby, you look like a goddess with that pregnant belly. I want to make love to you all the time." I touch her fingers and she lets me go, my body burning with desire for my wife. My head dips down to kiss her swollen stomach and her hips jerk. I trail my hot lips all over the surface of her smooth belly. My fingers sink into her lush hips, loving the extra weight she's put on during her second pregnancy. "I can't believe we're having another child. Kayden's going to be a big brother."

"Mmmm..." My wife's fingers thrust into my hair, loving the way I worship her fertile body. "Though my favorite part of the pregnancy was being bred by my husband. I can never get enough of you coming inside me."

"That's my favorite too, baby." I kiss her distended belly button, moving my lips up to kiss the sensitive underside of her plump breasts. She takes a deep breath in, her massive milkers on full display. Her teats are large as saucers, dark and swollen from making milk. Her nipples harden when I brush a finger over them, tingling for more. Little veins spread out from her teats, covering her breasts, and making me want to lick and suck on them.. When I cup her mounds, she moans.

"Do your tits hurt, baby?" I ask, gently massaging her achy, tender breasts. I know she gets very sensitive when she's engorged, and as her husband, it's my duty to relieve her when she's hurting. My big hands cover her massive mounds that are dangling like melons. I scissor my fingers around her swollen tips, massaging them to get her milk flowing.

"That feels so good. I've been engorged all day. Kayden doesn't need my milk anymore, and I forgot to pump." She opens her eyes, watching the first beads of milk form on her teats. I lick my lips, aching to taste her sweet cream. Our eyes meet and my wife bites her lower lip. "I thought my husband could milk me today."

"Damn, baby, you always have the best ideas." I lower my head, licking one tender nipple with my tongue.

"God, that feels so good." Elsie threads her fingers in my hair and pulls me closer to her breast. I lick the beads of milk leaking steadily from her wet tips, tasting her sweet cream.

"You taste like honey, baby girl." I flick my tongue against her aroused bud, making her whine with pleasure. "Daddy wants to suck on these big Mommy milkers for dessert."

"Yes, Daddy," she whines. "Milk me like I'm your slut. I want to feed you my cream straight from the source." She doesn't have to ask twice. My hot mouth closes around one squishy tip and I suck hard. Her letdown hits like a wave, making her entire body shiver. A burst of sweet cream hits my mouth and I gulp it down hungrily, feeling her sweetness slide down my throat. I lick and tease her puffy teat, pulling it deeper into my mouth as I drain her with hard, desperate sucks. Her nails drag on my scalp, and my wife holds me securely between her massive tits, giving herself to me as I swallow her milk. There's so much of it that it spills from the sides of my mouth, running down her massive belly. "Oh god…yes…just like that…." Her body fills with goosebumps, her pussy leaking moisture as I drain one breast.

When I look up, there's cream all over my lips, but I'm nowhere near done. Elsie smiles at me, panting. Her legs wind around my ass, her toes teasing my balls as I take her other nipple into my mouth and suck. My fingers trail down her belly, slipping between her legs, where I find her dripping cunt all swollen and ready to take my cock. My fingers tease her clit and she gasps, arching her back and thrusting her nipple deeper into my hungry mouth. Cream flows out from everywhere, covering the bedsheet and her body in trails of white. There's so much of it that I can't drink it all down, but I won't stop milking her achy tits until she's feeling better. When I plop her nipple out of my mouth, I know she's ready to be fucked.

"Get on all fours and show me your sexy ass, wife. I want to pound that pussy from behind and fill you with my seed like you're my breeding slut."

Elsie groans. She's really into breeding and dirty talk, and I love making my wife happy. She quickly gets onto all fours, her tender breasts hanging down like melons and dripping drops of cream steadily onto the bedsheet as she thrusts her ass up in the air. Her pregnant bump hangs low, making her look so damn sexy. My cock is on fire, aching to bury itself in her sweet, slick pussy. I slap her ass and watch it jiggle as she presents her wet, pink pussy to me, all bare and ready to be fucked.

"Fuck me, husband," she cries. "My pussy is aching for your cock so bad."

"Mmmm..." I run the wet head of my cock all over her swollen lips, enjoying when her hands shake. "I'm never going to get tired of coming inside my baby girl's pussy. Look how perfect it is. Every time I thrust into that needy little hole and fill you up, it feels so good." I drag my tip to her opening and slide in.

"Yes!" Elsie cries out as I fill her up in one stroke. She's all wet and willing, her cunt vacuuming my cock in. I feel her walls stretch and ripple all around me. She's still so tight, so perfectly open for her man.

"God, you're the best," she cries. "I love how you stretch my little cunt, Ronan."

"Baby, your body is perfection." I lean lower, kissing her spine. The scars of her mother's abuse have faded, and I'm so glad I took her away from that house. I kiss the little scars that remain, making her pussy hungry for my cock with every brush of my lips against her skin.

"Ronan..." Elsie shivers, loving it when I kiss her scars, reminding her of the first time I touched her in her bedroom.

"I love making love to you, Mrs. Jackson." I begin moving inside her, pounding her pussy hard. I thrust back into her cunt, watching her entire body shake with pleasure. Her fat tits and baby bump bounce as I drill her hand from the back. Burying my hands into her hips, I hold her tight, caressing her swollen stomach as I fuck her senseless. "And I love it when you take my cock like a good girl."

My tip grazes her G-spot and she grips the bedsheets hard. My balls slap against her ass, my shaft squelching in and out of her pregnant pussy as I fuck my wife to oblivion. My vision blurs when her pussy grips me hard, and I know she's close to coming.

"Come for me, baby girl. I want to feel that fertile little pussy choke my dick." I fuck her hard and fast, touching the womb that I bred so good. When I scrape against her sweet spot once more, the friction makes us both explode.

Elsie comes with a loud cry, her pussy contracting around my fat dick and choking every drop of pleasure out of me. I orgasm inside her, my veins burning with pleasure as I feel her pussy ripple and spasm around my cock, milking me for my seed. My balls empty into her cunt, filling her with hot, thick ropes of cum. Elsie cries, loving the feel of my cum filling up her empty vessel.

"Oh my god..." Her fleshy walls grip me hard. "I love it

when you come inside me, Ronan. It makes me feel like yours."

"Me too, baby. I love breeding the cunt I own." I squeeze her hips, massaging her fat stomach as we drift away in clouds of bliss.

Several moments later, she's lying on my chest, all sweaty and milky and drained from the orgasm. I pull her close to my naked body, touching her belly and kissing her temple as we both catch our breaths. Her juices coat my cock, reminding me of the first time I fucked her.

"That was amazing," she says. "I can't believe sex between us is still so good. My mom and dad lost interest in each other pretty quickly."

"That's never going to be us." I grab her hips and pull her close to me, kissing her hair. "I told you, no matter how your body changes, I'll always love you."

Elsie looks up, her blue eyes shimmering with tears. "I know. I'm the luckiest girl in the world because you're mine." I lean down, brushing my lips against hers.

"I love you, baby. You're the best decision of my life."

"I love you too," she whispers, her lips meeting and parting. "I'm so glad I fell for my tutor and married him." She opens her eyes and I kiss her nose. "My tutor, my stalker, and now my husband."

"I like the last one the most."

"Me too."

And then, we lose ourselves in each other for the rest of the night.

ABOUT THE AUTHOR

Jade Swallow is an author of super steamy novels. She loves reading and writing filthy tales featuring all kinds of kinks. Follow her on Instagram @authorjadeswallow for news about upcoming books.

Sign up for my newsletter here to get updates about my upcoming releases: subscribepage.io/eiSMM1

If you'd like to read my upcoming books, shorts, and/or support me, check out my Ream page: https://reamstories.com/jadeswallow

ALSO BY JADE SWALLOW

Want to read more books in the Dark Fantasies series?

Milkmaid for my Bully: A dark high school milking fantasy with pregnancy

Looking for more dark and steamy college-age romances by me? Check out this one:

Broken (Twisted Souls #1)

She's a serial killer on a mission, and he's her next target. But things get complicated when she begins falling for him.

Love Daddy kink, breeding, and milking? Check out these books:

Breeding the Babysitter: A forbidden age gap billionaire romance with pregnancy (Forbidden Daddies #1)

Mountain Daddy's Curvy Maid : A grumpy-sunshine age gap romance with pregnancy and lactation (Mountain Daddies #1)

Pregnant by the Mafia Boss : A forbidden age gap mafia romance with pregnancy (Mafia Daddies #1)

Lessons in Love with my Brother's Best Friend: A forbidden age gap erotica with pregnancy and BBW milking

Milked by my Best Friend's Mom : An age gap lesbian erotic novella

Looking for paranormal and omegaverse erotica? Check out these books by me:

The Vampire's Milkmaid: A gothic fated mates billionaire vampire romance with breeding, milking, and pregnancy (Paranormal Mates #1)

Stranded on the Shifter's Mountain: A Fated Mates Werewolf Shifter Romance with Breeding and Pregnancy (Paranormal Mates #2)

A Hucow Nanny for the Alpha Daddies: An age gap reverse harem fated mates omegaverse novella with pregnancy and milking (Omegaverse Daddies #1)

Alpha Daddy's Omega: An age gap pregnancy knotting and pregnant short story with arranged marriage (Omegaverse Daddies #2)

The Sea God's Fertile Bride : An age gap tentacle monster erotica (Married and Pregnant Monster Shorts #1)

Beauty and the Orc: An age gap orc daddy monster romance (Married and Pregnant Monster Shorts #2)

Short story bundles with milking, age gap, and breeding:

Summer Heat Series Bundle (Summer Heat #1-5)

Feeding Fantasies Box Set (Feeding Fantasies 1-5 + 2 bonus shorts)

Creamy and Pregnant Short Stories (Billionaires & Hucows #1-5)

Creamy Fantasies Box Set (Creamy Fantasies #1-5)